D0237982

ELLIE DAINES

Lolly Luck

ANDERSEN PRESS • LONDON

First published in 2012 by
Andersen Press Limited
20 Vauxhall Bridge Road
London SW1V 2SA
www.andersenpress.co.uk

4 6 8 10 9 7 5 3

British Library Cataloguing in Publication Data available.

ISBN 978 1 84939 396 6

Printed and bound by CPI Group (UK) Ltd, Croydon, CR0 4YY

For Melanie

Chapter 1

I'd never seen my dad cry before. It certainly wasn't what I was expecting when I got home from school. It was a horrible end to what had started off as the perfect birthday. My morning had begun with a special birthday breakfast of French toast with crispy bacon, and a fruit salad topped off with strawberry yoghurt. My favourite. Mum had put all my birthday cards into a neat little pile next to my presents and had tied a *Happy Birthday* balloon to my chair. But straightaway I could tell that one present was missing; the present I'd been looking forward to the most – my brilliant new bike. I knew my parents had bought me a bike. They'd been whispering to each other for weeks and 'bike' was the word I always picked up. I'd wanted one for ages; a proper grown-up bike with gears, which hadn't been handed down from my sister, Zola, and wasn't covered in Barbie stickers.

Zola was already at the table having her breakfast, a yucky concoction of scrambled egg mashed up with baked beans. Even though I like baked beans and I absolutely adore scrambled egg, they *so* do not go together.

'Happy birthday, Lollipop,' said Mum, giving me a hug. 'I can't believe you're eleven today! You're growing up so fast. You excited?'

'Yeah, totally,' I replied. 'And today's going to be fantastic.'

'Oh, it will be, don't you worry. Your dad and I have got you a wonderful present. Dad's been called into work a bit early today, so we'll give it to you this evening. I hope that's OK?'

I smiled at Mum. 'Of course.' But, no, it *wasn't* OK. I wanted my bike at that precise minute and wasn't looking forward to waiting twelve torturous hours before I finally got to see it.

'Right then, I've got to scoot off myself. Enjoy your breakfast, birthday girl – and, Zola, no dawdling on the way to the bus stop,' said Mum, grabbing her handbag and looking pointedly at my sister. 'Make sure you and Lolly get to school on time.'

'Yes, Zola, no flirting with boys and making us late,' I mumbled, picking up a slice of French toast.

'Omigod that is such a lie,' said Zola, glaring at me. 'Just because it's your birthday, Lolly, it doesn't mean you can start showing off.'

'Girls!' Mum snapped. 'Can't the two of you get through a day without arguing?'

We sighed and nodded obediently, but as soon as Mum had left the room Zola was poking her tongue out, pieces of her vomit-looking breakfast falling onto her plate.

'Oh, grow up, Zola,' I hissed.

My sister is fourteen but sometimes it's like she's only four. I know Mum thinks we argue too much, but really we do get on and, to be honest, I don't think there's anyone else I'd want as my big sister. I can talk to Zola about anything, and ever since I was really little she's been there for me. When Zola was still at my primary school I could always count on her to back me up whenever my arch-enemy, Mariella Sneddon, tried to upset me with some snidy remark. All Zola needed to do was threaten Mariella with a wallop, which was enough to have her running scared.

'By the way, happy birthday, Lolly Loser,' said Zola, hurling a card and a little parcel at me.

Lolly Loser is Zola's horrid pet name for me, even though she knows I'm no loser. I'm Lolly Luck by name, lucky by nature. I'm the luckiest person I know, and the luckiest person everyone else knows. When I was eight I won a short-story competition at school and got fifteen pounds in book tokens. That same year I also won a magazine competition. The prize was actually something Zola wanted, but seeing how I'm the lucky one she entered my name instead of hers and won a make-up set, which she had to hide from Mum as she doesn't like us wearing make-up. And, of course, there have been all the birthday parties where I've beaten everyone else to the last seat in musical chairs and unwrapped the last parcel in pass the parcel. And for the past two years in a row it's been me who's scooped the top raffle prize at my school's Christmas fête. The first year I won *Ice Age* and *Ice Age 2* on DVD, and then just this Christmas I won a digital camera, which *so* got up Mariella's nose. She really couldn't handle the fact that I'd won again and she tried to say the whole thing was a fix and that I must have bribed one of the teachers to make sure it was my raffle ticket that got pulled out. The horrible cow even got her dad to talk to the head teacher, Mr Kingsley, so he could conduct an investigation into whether I'd cheated. Unfortunately for Mariella and her dad, Mr Kingsley took my side and told them I was simply lucky, just like my surname, and asked could they stop wasting his time with their 'wild accusations'. Mariella's spiteful thinks-she's-so-special face was a picture.

So, back to my luck. Well, another thing I'm lucky with is finding money – and I'm not just talking about coins, but actual notes. It's like they appear by magic right in front of me wherever I am: five-pound notes *and* ten-pound notes. And that's not all. I also have a very special ability – I dream about the winning lottery numbers, yes, really. It's happened twice, and each time three numbers out of the six actually came up. In the dreams I'm watching the lottery show on the telly when the balls with my numbers on suddenly tumble out of the machine. Luckily after both dreams I've remembered the numbers. I wrote them down and gave them to my mum and dad, Auntie Louise and Granny Doreen, and all of them won ten pounds both times. I also helped my auntie win money on a scratchcard. One day we were in the sweet shop and she told me to pick one of the containers with the cards in. I chose container number five and when she scratched off the card she got three lucky stars in a row and won a hundred pounds. She gave me twenty pounds from it to say thank you, which I popped straight into my piggy bank. Granny Doreen reckons I've got a gift. She says I'm psychic, although I'm not sure that I want to be as I've heard psychic people can see ghosts, and I never, ever want to see a ghost.

'Go on, open it,' said Zola as I added her card to the pile. 'I've put something special in there for you.'

I glanced at my sister suspiciously before picking up the card. But really I should've just given it straight back to her because as soon as I opened it a loud burp went off in my face. Then, in a drunk voice, the card wished me a happy birthday. Trust Zola!

'And the present, go on, open it,' she said, laughing loudly.

I narrowed my eyes at her as I unwrapped the present carefully in case it contained something gross too, but to my surprise her present was actually lovely. She'd bought me a silver bangle embossed with little flowers.

'Thanks, Zola!' I went round the table to give her a hug.

'Watch my hair.' She pretended to fuss over her cornrows that Mum had plaited the previous night. 'So do you think you'll wear it this evening?'

'Definitely,' I smiled.

We were planning to celebrate my birthday with a special dinner at a restaurant in the centre of town. It's called the Royal Tandoori, and I was really excited about going and trying their chilli sea bass, which Dad said tasted 'tremendous'. He'd had to book our table ages ago as the Royal Tandoori is always packed with customers. It's also very popular with celebrities, including my favourite singer Corey T. I had my fingers crossed that he'd be there later when we went.

'Do you reckon we'll see anyone famous tonight?' I asked Zola.

'You mean Corey T?' she replied, sniggering. 'You're obsessed with him, Lolly! I can't understand why. I mean, it's not as if the boy can actually sing, plus he's ugly.'

'No he's not, he's gorgeous,' I said. 'And he's the best singer out of all the singers in the world. And if he is at the restaurant tonight I'm going to get his autograph.'

*

After I'd finished eating my breakfast I opened my other cards and presents. Some of them had *Lollyanna* written on the front while the rest just said *Lolly*.

Lollyanna is my proper name, but everyone who knows me calls me Lolly. My name is made up, partly by Zola, of all people. My sister decided to give me half my name when she came to the hospital on a snowy January day to see me for the first time. I was all wrapped up in my snugly yellow blanket, my eyes squinting at her as she stared back saying 'lolly' again and again. Zola can't remember if it's true that she wanted me to be called Lolly or actually wanted me to have a lick of the lollipop she was holding at the time. Mum and Dad had planned to name me Anna after Mum's favourite auntie who died before Zola and I were born, but when Mum tried to explain this to my sister, Zola started screaming her head off, causing me and all the other newborns on the ward to burst out crying. So to get Zola to shut up, my parents promised her they'd combine both names to make a new one. And that's the short story of how I got to be called Lollyanna.

My card from Auntie Louise and her little girl Mariah had *Lolly* written on the envelope and my auntie had coloured in two yellow circles over the two ‘l’s to look like lollipops. Inside the card was a thirty-pound gift card for New Look, which made me very happy as I wanted some new clothes. Even though Mariah’s only three months old and can’t talk yet, she’s my favourite cousin. She’s such a cutie and always giggles when you tickle her feet. They lived with us for a bit when Auntie Louise split up with Uncle Clive. It was brilliant having a baby around, although I don’t think it was much fun for Auntie Louise. She cried more than Mariah, all because Uncle Clive had dumped her for another woman.

I opened Granny Doreen’s present next. She’d bought me the same present she gets me every birthday – a pack of knickers. Unfortunately my gran isn’t very imaginative when it comes to presents and always buys knickers for the women and girls in my family. My present from Uncle Finn, Auntie Trish and my twin cousins Calvin and Curtis was much better. They’d got me a Corey T photo book with lots of stunning pictures of him inside, along with a Corey T calendar. The last card in the pile was from Great-Uncle Ernest and was in a large silver envelope. As I opened it, I couldn’t believe my eyes – loads of twenty-pound notes scattered over my plate.

Zola was just as shocked. 'Has Great-Uncle Ernest robbed a bank, or something?' she gasped.

We counted the money slowly and couldn't believe it. *Three hundred pounds!* Then we counted it again. Yes, it was three hundred pounds. Great-Uncle Ernest was always very generous, but this was crazy. Usually he'd slot in a fifty-pound note, so I guess he must have been in a pretty good mood to have given me all this. I wish I could've said thank you, but I've never actually met Great-Uncle Ernest, or even spoken to him. Neither has Dad or Zola. He lives in an old people's home in Southend but nobody ever sees him because he doesn't like having visitors. One thing I do know, though, is that Great-Uncle Ernest never forgets my birthday, and I get money at Christmas too.

'Why does Great-Uncle Ernest give you money and never me? He treats me like I'm invisible, it's so unfair!' huffed Zola.

'Well maybe he'll remember your birthday next year,' I replied, feeling sorry for my sister. But deep down, we both knew Great-Uncle Ernest probably wouldn't remember. He's never sent Zola cards or money for her birthday or Christmas even though my mum's written to him heaps of times to remind him she has two daughters not one. But for some reason Great-Uncle Ernest just keeps forgetting. Mum reckons it's because he's old. Great-Uncle Ernest is in his eighties. Still, I'm always pleased to receive a card from him and to show my appreciation I like to make Great-Uncle Ernest a paper fan every Christmas, which my mum posts to him. And with the fan, she also includes a recent photo of me.

I collect fans too, from all over the world. I buy them when we go on holiday, and so far I have fans from St Lucia, Disney World, Spain and Cyprus. My favourite is the one from Spain, it has a picture of a man and a woman dancing on it. In the picture the woman is wearing a long red dress and her black hair is slicked back into a bun. The man is wearing a brown suit and is gazing into the woman's eyes. It's such a romantic picture, and sometimes I like to imagine that I'm the woman and the man is Corey T.

Just like every birthday since I was five, I arrived at school armed with chocolates. Mum had bought me a tin of Quality Street to share with my class and as usual it was the yellow ones that went first, my absolute favourite.

At break time my best friend, Nancy, gave me a card and present. She'd bought me a lovely tiny teddy bear that was wearing a yellow bow tie. Nancy's been my best friend ever since I fell out with my former best friend, Mariella, in Year Three. We used to really get on, Mariella and me, and would share each other's clothes and go to each other's houses for sleepovers. But all of that ended when she accused me of stealing her sparkly butterfly clip; a clip she said had real diamonds in it and had once belonged to some dead film star who was friends with her gran. She went round telling everyone I was a thief – and it was all because Mr Kingsley chose me to read my poem at the Christmas concert and not her and she was jealous. I've never stolen anything in my life, but Mariella had me feeling like a right criminal, plus she threatened to get her dad to call the police on me. For weeks she went on and on about the clip, so much so that other kids in our class started to hide their pens and pencils whenever I came near. I lost so many mates because of her. So after that, as far as I was concerned, Mariella Sneddon was no longer my friend.

The only person who didn't hide their things from me was Nancy. In fact, she was more than happy to share her stuff, and for a while was the only person who'd hang out with me at break and lunch time. I'm glad Nancy's my best friend. I just wish I'd made the effort to get to know her way back in Reception. The problem was, she was always so quiet and didn't seem to want to talk to anybody. At first I thought she was being stuck up. But the reason she was like that was because she had a lot on her mind. Her parents were going through a divorce and poor Nancy was playing piggy in the middle as they fought over her custody. She wasn't being stuck up at all. Nancy's actually the least stuck-up person I know. She's very kind, very thoughtful and has never ever accused me of being a thief.

We have a lot in common, Nancy and me. We both love Corey T, the colour yellow and our favourite films are *The Princess and the Frog*, *Night at the Museum* and *Back to the Future*, the first and second film (but not the third film). We have the same 'sister twist' hairstyles and both play in the school netball team. I play goal attack, Nancy plays centre. And our sleepovers are way better than any of the sleepovers I had with Mariella. I prefer going to Nancy's house, though, as she has these two sweet bunny rabbits called Cheese and

Pickle who'll hop into your arms like little acrobats, chomping away on the carrots and lettuce you feed them. Nancy lives with her mum, Diane, who's really nice and lets us stay up really late when our sleepovers are on a Friday or Saturday night. It's great because we get to eat midnight snacks and sing songs Nancy's written herself. Nancy wants to be a singer/songwriter when she grows up and I think she'll be very successful as her voice is amazing.

When I grow up I think I'll be an events manager like my mum. Her job is *soooo* cool, especially when she gets to organise these really glamorous parties, which are held in swish hotels and art galleries. Plus, all the party guests get to drink champagne and eat canapés. Sometimes, if there are any canapés left over, Mum will bring them home, which is always awesome because they'll be miniature versions of my favourite foods, like fish and chips and toad-in-the-hole. One time Mum even brought home these crisps that had been made out of pigs' ears, but I didn't like them. Zola did, though.

'Thanks for the present,' I said to Nancy, stroking the belly of my new teddy bear.

'That's OK. So, did you get your bike?'

I shook my head. 'No, I'm getting it tonight.

My mum and dad still think I don't know, but I'm going to pretend to be totally surprised.'

I made Nancy laugh as I showed her the astonished face I was planning to pull, my mouth open as wide as the *Titanic* and my eyes literally popping out of my head.

All day I couldn't stop thinking about my bike, imagining myself riding it down my road and all the way up to the park on Crofton Lane. When the final bell went my heart was beating so fast I thought I might actually faint from all the excitement.

But when Zola and I got home, Mum was on the sofa with Dad sitting opposite, his hands cupped together and his head bowed. At first I was surprised to see him home so early as he's never normally in until about seven. But when he looked up at me, his eyes puffy and red, I knew something terrible had happened.

'What is it, Dad?' I asked worriedly.

'I'm sorry, girls, but I've got some bad news,' he said, wiping his eyes with a tissue. 'It's my boss – he's had to let me go. I've lost my job.'

And there it was – my eleventh birthday, a birthday which I thought was going to be my best ever, had turned into my worst.

Chapter 2

I felt really scared after Dad told us he'd lost his job, and when my parents gave me my bike it didn't feel quite so special any more. And we didn't go to the Royal Tandoori. No one really felt like it, so Mum ordered a takeaway pizza, but I could hardly eat any of mine, my stomach feeling sore with all the worry.

Dad's company, Havers and Cole, had made him redundant. At first I wasn't sure what making someone redundant was, but Dad quickly explained that it's when a company gets rid of people they can't afford to keep on and they give them some money called a redundancy package to sort of say sorry for giving them the boot. Dad said the company had been losing money so that's why they'd had to do this. I felt like ringing up Dad's bosses, Mr Havers and Mr Cole, to see if they needed any help with finding their missing money so my dad could get his job back. But Dad said the money would never be recovered, it was simply lost for ever.

My dad worked as a financial analyst and his job involved having to do lots of difficult sums. I'm sure he found the sums easy as he's a genius when it comes to maths. I can ask my dad any maths question and he'll always give me the answer quicker than a calculator.

'And to think I did so much for that company,' said Dad, throwing down a slice of pizza. 'I was working fourteen hours a day when they were chasing that big deal with the American bank. I didn't get to see any of you as I was practically living at the office. I knew they were planning redundancies, but my manager assured me my job would be safe. He said I had nothing to worry about, I should've known he'd stab me in the back.'

'How much redundancy money do you think you'll get?' Mum asked.

'Well I've only been there for two and a half

years, so I doubt I'll get the same as Jake,' said Dad solemnly. 'The poor sod gave thirty years to that company. You should've seen his face, love, when they gave him the news. I've never seen a man more devastated.'

'Make sure you speak to the Job Centre tomorrow. We won't get by on just my wages,' said Mum. 'We seriously need two salaries coming in, Austin. And I think we'd better forget about going to Ghana in the summer, there's no way we'll be able to afford it now.'

'I'll get another job, love. Please don't fret about the holiday.'

'We *are* going to be all right for money, though, aren't we?' Zola asked as her eyes shuffled over to where I was sitting. 'Lolly's bike must have cost you loads, are you sure we can afford it? Cos she can always get a bike next year, can't you, Lolly? And I hardly ever play with my Xbox, so you could sell that too.'

Suddenly I felt really guilty. I didn't want to have to give back my bike, not when I'd only just got it. But I didn't want my family to not have any money.

'Yeah. Sure. I can get a bike next year,' I mumbled. 'I don't mind if you want to take it back.'

'No, Lolly. That bike is your birthday present,' Dad insisted. 'Your mum and I know how much you've wanted one so there's no way on earth we'd take it away from you. And there's no need for us to sell your Xbox, either, Zola.'

Mum nodded her head in agreement.

'We'll be OK for money. We just have to be a bit more careful, that's all. I don't want any of you worrying that we haven't got enough,' said Dad.

Mum gave him a hug. 'We love you, don't we, girls? Someone as clever as you, I'm sure you'll have a new job in no time.'

'Thanks, love. The first thing I'll do tomorrow is call some recruitment agencies.'

'What are they, Dad?' I asked.

'People who help others find jobs.'

'I'll help you find a job if you want,' I said, trying to be helpful.

He smiled gently. 'Thanks, Lollipop, but I think I'll be OK finding a job myself. I'm Austin Luck, remember – with a surname like mine something's bound to turn up.'

Despite Dad telling us not to worry I couldn't help it, and I didn't sleep a wink that night, a long train of questions *choo-chooing* through my mind. What if Dad couldn't find a job? What then? How would we pay for food? How would we pay the heating bills? Our house would be *freeeeeezing* if we couldn't have the heating on.

I decided to see if Zola had any answers. But as it was the middle of the night she wasn't too pleased to see me. She even let out a little scream.

'What is it, Loser? What do you want?' she croaked, rubbing her eyes as I switched on her bedroom light.

'I can't sleep, Zola. I'm worried.'

'Worried? About what?'

'Dad.'

'Oh,' she muttered, and slowly heaved herself up.

'I'm scared he won't find another job,' I said all in a panic. 'And if he doesn't, we might not have any money for anything. We won't be able to buy clothes or go on school trips, and we might not even have enough money to buy food. Mum's always complaining about how pricey food is. We might have to start eating beans and rice like those people in that jungle show on telly.'

'You think too much,' said Zola, yawning. 'I do understand why you're worried. But trust me, we're not going to starve.'

'Do you think I should give Mum and Dad the money Great-Uncle Ernest gave me?'

Zola shrugged, 'I guess you could . . .' But then she shook her head. 'No, Lolly, that money's yours to keep. And, besides, you heard Dad, he doesn't want us to worry. Look, I'm sure things will be OK.'

As I sloped off back to my room I really hoped Zola was right, that things would be OK.

Only they weren't.

At first it was brilliant having Dad at home all the time. Every morning he'd walk me and Zola to the bus stop and we'd chat about loads of things, from how badly his football team were doing to films we wanted to see at the cinema. Then, when we got in from school, Dad would help us with our homework and sometimes take me to the park so I could have a ride on my bike. He even made chocolate brownies with us, which wasn't something he'd normally do since he wasn't very good at baking. But they turned out well. However after about three weeks of not having a job, things started to change. It was like Dad had suddenly become a different person, a totally miserable, moody person. He began to have long lie-ins, which meant neither Zola nor I got to see him before we left for school. Then, when we got home, he was either sitting at the computer applying for jobs over the internet or was on the phone chatting to recruitment agencies. And wherever he went, his mobile and the house phone went too, because when he wasn't talking on one of them, he was waiting for them to ring. He even started to take the phones with him to the toilet.

'I can't miss a single call,' he'd say. 'It might be a recruitment consultant who wants to talk to me about a new role that's come in.'

To begin with he'd only searched for jobs during the day, but quickly his entire time had become occupied with finding one. And it was like he didn't want to talk to us any more. He stopped asking Zola and me how school was going and stopped helping us with our homework, and he stopped taking me to the park. He'd tell Zola to go with me, but most of the time she didn't want to, which meant the only place I got to ride my bike was up and down our road. Plus, he didn't want to make any more chocolate brownies.

And when I did manage to get a conversation out of Dad, nothing he said ever seemed to make any sense.

'I feel like I'm in a pool filled with quicksand,

and as much as I try to pull myself out, I'm still stuck,' he said to me one day when I asked him how he was feeling.

The other stuff that came out of Dad's mouth would mostly be a rant about the Job Centre and the recruitment consultants that were 'wasting his time' by continually asking him if he was looking for a job but not actually doing anything to help him *find* a job. Mum found it tricky to get a conversation out of him too, and he hardly ever joined us at the dining table for dinner, preferring to sit by himself in the living room; one eye on the telly, the other eye on the phones. Then when one of the phones eventually rang, it was like two electrical heart pads had been placed against Dad's chest, shocking him back to life, his gloomy face lighting up as he'd launch to answer it. But more often his excitement would turn into disappointment when he realised it wasn't a recruitment consultant at the other end but Granny Doreen telling him to hurry along with finding a job.

I tried to cheer Dad up by making him some paper fans. I had to use old newspapers and magazines, though, as Dad wouldn't let me use the printer paper because that was reserved for his CVs. I decorated the fans with sticky stars and glitter, and drew on smiley faces. But unfortunately they didn't do the trick – Dad stayed miserable.

I would've loved for my luck to have rubbed off on Dad, but it probably wouldn't have worked cos I wasn't feeling too lucky myself. I hadn't spotted any money on the ground in ages and I so wanted to find some to help my parents out. On top of all that I'd had some sad news of my own. Mrs Avery, my favourite teacher ever, was going on maternity leave in a few months' time. A supply teacher would be filling in for her and none of my class was looking forward to it. I was worried the supply teacher would be some grumpy-pants who liked sending kids out of the room if they dared to interrupt while they were speaking. My Year Four teacher, Mrs Barnes, had been like that and at one point it felt like I was spending more time sitting in the corridor than sitting at my desk.

A few of us had formed a group to make Mrs Avery's leaving card. We'd decided to meet up once a week at lunch time to make it – a picture of a baby boy because that's what Mrs Avery had told us she was expecting. Big-mouth Mariella had put herself in charge of the group, and also the list that we had to put our names on to do certain parts of the picture. Sanjay Kumar was doing the baby's left eye;

Kayla Kennedy, the right eye; Alice Chang would be doing the nose and mouth; Ian Metcalf, the ears; Dominique Foster, the body; and I was planning to do the flowerbed that the baby would be sitting in. But that cow Mariella went and deliberately crossed my name out, replacing it with the name of her newest best friend, Trinity Hibbard.

'No offence,' she said to me at the first card-making session, 'but I think Trinity will do a nicer job of the flowerbed. She's very creative, you know, she'll make the flowers look exquisite.'

I was ready to have it out with Mariella, tell her what I thought of her selfish, snotty attitude, but Nancy calmly persuaded me not to. So I ended up getting lumbered with drawing the baby's hair, which I wasn't the least bit happy about. Still, I tried to make the best of it, and brought in my special felt-tip pens to do yellow tufts of hair with a few orange strands thrown in as Mrs Avery has a few gingery bits in her hair. I thought it looked lovely until Mariella stuck her nose in and started ranting and raving that I'd made the baby look like he'd been given an electric shock. The next thing I knew she was cutting out a magazine picture of some woman's hair and had gone and stuck it over the baby's head.

Nancy had decided to get involved in the card-making sessions when she found out her latest crush, Kofi Adu, would be drawing the baby's bottle. Mariella had given Nancy the job of doing the baby's nappy. But she only came to three sessions and spent most of her time staring at Kofi and turning her head away whenever he looked back at her. The baby's nappy was made out of a white flannel that Nancy had brought in from home, it had a safety pin stuck to it using Blu-Tack, which apparently was what mums used to do in the olden days before they had Pampers.

One day Wayne Clements offered to pour some apple juice over the nappy to make it look more realistic, which had Mariella practically steaming at the ears like some crazy cartoon character.

'Urgh, that's rank! There's no way you're pouring anything over that nappy!' she screamed. 'Do you actually have a brain, Wayne, or were you just born stupid?'

Wayne was only trying to make himself useful, but the way Mariella was carrying on you'd think he'd gone and murdered somebody. I was seriously getting fed up with her nasty attitude, so much so that part of me wished I'd never got involved in making Mrs Avery's card in the first place.

At home things were getting worse with Mum regularly on Dad's case for not helping her around the house.

'You're leaving me to do everything, Austin,' she'd say. 'It's not fair, especially when you've been here all day. Surely it wouldn't have taken you two minutes to put out the rubbish or pick up some milk from the corner shop.'

'I don't have the time to do those things, Marion. I need to keep up my job search so I can get myself some interviews.'

Sadly Dad didn't get invited to any interviews. He applied for tons of jobs, but all he got back were rejections or simply no answer at all. And it was awful because he just became more and more disheartened. Very quickly the cheerful, happy-go-lucky Dad I was used to began to disappear right in front of my eyes.

Chapter 3

Before Dad lost his job my parents hardly ever argued. They always seemed far too happy to be getting into silly squabbles like Zola and I did. But after Dad was made redundant that all changed. One day they had an enormous row after Dad didn't take Mum out for dinner.

She'd really been looking forward to their evening out at an Italian restaurant. Before she left for work in the morning, she'd put on her special shoes. They're covered in red sequins just like the ruby slippers in *The Wizard of Oz*. But when Mum called Dad's mobile in the evening, he was still at home, sitting at the computer with no intention of shifting. And from the way he was holding the phone and scrunching his eyes I could tell she was giving him an earful.

Mum was livid when she got in, and she looked like she'd been crying too. I think Zola could tell an argument was coming cos she quickly left saying she was going to her friend Gita's house to return a DVD she'd borrowed.

'You had me waiting in the restaurant for over an hour!' Mum snapped.

'I haven't got time to be sitting around eating pasta, Marion. I have jobs to apply for,' Dad bit back. 'Or would you prefer me to stay unemployed?'

'Of course I don't want you to be unemployed. But it was your idea we go out. I thought you would've appreciated having some time away from the computer.'

'I have to find a job.'

'So you keep telling me. Well, the supermarket on the high street is looking for staff. Why don't you go there tomorrow and pick up an application form?'

Dad snorted. 'I'm a financial analyst, Marion, not a checkout boy.'

'But it's work, love, paid work and you've been unemployed for more than two months,' said Mum, flicking her dreadlocks over her shoulder. 'The redundancy money's gone, and if you haven't forgotten we do still have a mortgage to pay. You really need a job *now*, Austin. I don't want us ending up on the streets.'

'We might have to live on the streets!' I gasped.

'No, Lolly, we're not going to live on the streets,' said Dad, shaking his head at Mum.

'Says the man who the last time I checked doesn't have a job to actually keep a roof over our heads,' she hissed.

'Marion, I will find a job. But I'm telling you it is not going to be in a supermarket. I've worked too hard building up a career to throw it all away and sit at a till listening to little old ladies going on about their arthritis and the war.'

'But you wouldn't have to work in the supermarket for ever, Austin. It'd just be until you find something else.'

'Will you stop nagging me, woman!' spluttered Dad.

'I'm not nagging you! I just want you to sort your life out!'

'Would you like a cup of tea?' I said, standing in-between my parents. I hated them arguing like this. I wanted it to stop. 'Maybe you and Dad can go out on Saturday instead?'

Mum flopped down onto the sofa. 'Your father will be too busy looking for a job to take me out on Saturday, or any other day, for that matter.'

She put her face in her hands as she took a few moments to compose herself. Then she breathed deeply, put her hands on her lap and looked straight at Dad. 'Right, just to let you know, I'm going into the kitchen to make myself something to eat then I'll be having my dinner in our bedroom.'

Dad shrugged his shoulders. 'Do what you like.'

Mum got up quickly, screwing her lips together as she stormed out the room.

'Sorry you had to hear that, Lollipop,' Dad apologised.

'Will we really end up on the streets like Mum said?'

'No, Lollipop, and I'll never let that happen. Your mother was just trying to scare me into taking some silly job that I don't want,' said Dad. 'I know things haven't been going well, but I do have a feeling my luck is about to turn. Someone's going to want to see me for an interview, I'm sure of it. I might even get the call tomorrow. I'm Luck by name, lucky by nature. Isn't that what you always say, Lolly?'

I nodded slowly.

But I should have known that it was going to take a lot more than a catchphrase to make my dad lucky, because sometimes when your luck's gone, it's really gone.

The next day Dad didn't get up early like Mum had wanted. She was seriously cross and was banging things about as she made my and Zola's breakfast.

'What's wrong with Mum?' asked Zola in a low voice.

'She's angry with Dad,' I told her, then quietly explained what she'd missed last night.

When Mum left for work, she slammed the door really hard, which I know was for Dad's benefit, but unfortunately it didn't work. He was still fast asleep when Zola and I poked our heads round their bedroom door, his mouth opening and closing like a goldfish.

'Do you think we should wake him?' I whispered.

'No. I don't think he'll be too pleased if we do,' said Zola as she closed the door again. So we left Dad to enjoy the rest of his sleep and got ourselves off to school.

On the bus we bumped into our next-door neighbours, Mr and Mrs Papathomas. They're pretty old, but really nice, and ever since Zola and I helped them to find their cat, Cleo, when she went missing they've continued to reward us by dropping round these lovely pastries called baklava. They asked about Dad.

'We don't see him going to work any more,' said Mr Papathomas.

'He's taking some time off,' Zola responded, using the exact words Dad had told us to say if anyone asked after him. For some reason he didn't want people to know he was unemployed.

'He deserves a holiday. I know he works very hard,' said Mr Papathomas, flashing his usual cheery smile. 'One day he'll get to retire like us and he'll have lots and lots of time to do all the things he loves. Life really is more wonderful when you get to our age.'

He smiled again, this time at his wife, who looked back adoringly. Softly, she started to sing a Greek song, her husband joining in.

And I don't know why, but all of a sudden I found myself feeling really sad. Maybe it was because they reminded me of how Mum and Dad used to be. They were always singing to each other, doing duets and stuff. But that was when Dad had a job.

I was still a bit sad when I got to school, and as soon as I sat down at my desk it seemed like I was in for a terrible day. First, my results from Monday's spelling test were totally awful. I only got five words correct out of twenty, which had to be my lowest ever score in a spelling test. Then, just after morning break as I was going back to class, I tripped and fell, scraping my knee. But what made things worse was that I could hear Mariella creasing up with laughter in the background. Then at lunch time I accidentally splashed orange juice all over my school shirt. I looked a right mess and I couldn't wait for the day to end.

Thankfully things got a lot better when Mrs Avery told the class about the play we'd be doing at the end of the summer term. She wouldn't be here by then, but she promised to come back and see it. It was going to be modern version of *Pollyanna*, a book I'd read when I was in Year Five. It's about an orphan girl who has to live with her grumpy aunt in this miserable town, but because Pollyanna is a very happy person, she's able to make everyone else in the town feel happy too, and see the positive side of every situation. But unfortunately she gets hit by a car and all her optimism disappears as she can't walk. The people in the town come and visit her and let her know how much her positivity has helped them, which makes Pollyanna feel much better and optimistic again.

Straightaway I decided that I wanted to play Pollyanna since there were a few things I had in common with her. Not only did our names sound alike but we were both optimistic people who enjoyed cheering others up.

'So are you going to audition for the play?' asked Nancy as we stood against the sinks in the girls' toilets during afternoon break.

I nodded. 'Definitely. I want to be Pollyanna.'

'That's great, Lolly. I think you'd make a fab Pollyanna,' she said. 'I think I might audition too. I wouldn't mind playing Aunt Polly.'

'Brilliant! I'd love us to both be in the play,' I said. 'I know Mariella will probably want the part of Pollyanna, but I'm praying Mrs Avery gives it to me.'

'I think you're right, she *will* want the part,' Nancy agreed. 'There's no way Mariella will want to miss out on being the centre of attention seeing as it's her favourite place in the whole wide world.'

We giggled. 'Yeah, and I bet if she does get the role she'll be showing off right up until the performance,' I said, then did my best impression of

Mariella. 'Ooh, look at me, look at me. My name's Mariella and I'm soooo amazing, and when I'm older I'm going to be soooo famous and soooo rich.'

We laughed again.

'How's your dad doing? Has he found a job yet?' asked Nancy.

I shook my head. 'He's still looking. My mum wants him to get a job in a supermarket, but he's dead against it. They had a really big argument last night.'

'That's how it starts,' said Nancy.

'What starts?'

'First come the arguments, then it's the divorce. That's how it was with my mum and dad.'

'But I don't want my parents to get divorced!' My heart began to race and suddenly I felt really queasy. I hadn't thought that my parents' arguing might lead to them breaking up. I gripped the sink to steady myself.

'Sorry, no. I'm sure your parents won't split up, Lolly,' said Nancy, putting a hand on my shoulder. 'It's not as if your dad is like how mine used to be, driving my mum crazy buying expensive gadgets that we didn't need.'

'But what if they've stopped loving each other? All they ever seem to do these days is argue. And last night my mum said we might have to live on the streets if Dad doesn't find a job soon. So not only will I end up with divorced parents but I might have to live in a cardboard box too.' I began to sob.

'I'm sorry, Zola but we just can't renew your mobile phone contract,' said Dad to my sister when we both got home from school.

Zola was mortified, of course, and although Dad told her it was only a 'temporary measure' she begged him to change his mind. And I could see why. There had been a lot of 'temporary measures' in our house recently, none of them good. Mum had *temporarily* stopped buying the tomato ketchup Zola and I liked and started buying the supermarket brand instead, which was nowhere near as nice. Plus, the cream cheese and smoked salmon sandwiches she'd make for my lunch had *temporarily* become cream cheese without smoked salmon, or cream cheese with cucumber, as salmon was now too expensive. Dad had *temporarily* stopped ordering the newspaper we had delivered each morning, which meant Zola and I had to go without our daily fix of celebrity gossip. And my parents had *temporarily* cancelled our Sky TV subscription. For me this was the hardest 'temporary measure' of all as it meant I couldn't watch my favourite shows on Nickelodeon and the Disney Channel.

'Of course, when I do get a job then we will be able to start paying for your calls again,' said Dad.

'But when are you going to *get* this job, Dad?' said Zola, sounding like Mum. 'I'll become a social outcast if I can't to speak to my friends.'

'That's nonsense, Zola, and you know it,' Dad answered, pretending to swat her with his hand. 'Every month you exceed the limit that we've set you and I'm afraid it's just become too costly for us to carry on paying.'

'Then I'll stay within my limit. Please, Dad, please let me keep my phone.'

Dad shook his head. 'I'm sorry, but we need to use the money for other things, such as paying the household bills. And besides, maybe it'll do you some good detaching yourself from that phone for a while. You spend too much time on it as it is. It's your homework you need to be concentrating on after school, not chatting to Gita who you already see every day.'

But Zola just rolled her eyes and stomped off out of the room.

Dad looked hurt.

'She didn't mean to be like that,' I said and gave Dad a hug to cheer him up. 'She does understand that you and Mum don't have the money.'

'Thanks, sweetheart,' he replied, kissing me on the forehead. 'I know things have been tough for us recently but it will all get better.'

I had my audition for the play two weeks later. It was a Friday morning and Dad was up bright and early for a change. He was fussing over a CV he'd printed off and was desperate for Mum to take a look at it as he didn't trust the spell check on the computer.

'Please, Marion; I really need you to look at this,' he said. 'It'll only take a minute, love.'

'No, Austin. I can't be late for work so just get someone else to do it,' snapped Mum as she buttoned up her coat. 'Maybe that "astrologer" woman will look at it for you,' she added, wiggling two fingers in the air when she said 'astrologer'.

Dad had recently got into astrology, despite telling me and Zola for years that the whole thing was a pile of poop. He'd decided to call an astrologer and have his horoscope read to find out if some luck was about to come his way. But the astrologer's number was one of those telephone lines that cost a fortune to ring and when Mum found out they had a huge row.

'Heaven knows the amount of money you ran up phoning that "astrologer" (finger wiggle),' she was shouting. 'You know we've had to make cuts to our household finances just to keep us afloat, but there you are happily giving our money away to some woman who reckons she can read the stars.'

Dad had tried his best to convince Mum that calling the astrologer was a good thing because apparently the sun was about to move into his tenth house of career, which meant he'd be receiving a call about a job interview within two days.

Two days passed, and then a week, but Dad didn't get called by any recruitment consultant. The astrologer had been lying. When the phone bill arrived Mum went mad and my parents haven't spoken much to each other since.

After Mum had left for work, Dad turned to Zola who was eating a bowl of cornflakes. 'Zola, honey, can you take a look at my CV and my cover letter, please?'

'I can't, Dad, I'll be late as well,' she replied.

Dad frowned but nodded his head. 'Ignore me. I'm just getting myself into a silly panic. Anyway, you girls have a good day and, Lolly, good luck with your audition.'

'Thanks, Dad,' I said.

'And don't feel nervous, I'm sure you'll do just fine, Lollipop. I have every confidence that you'll get the starring role. We could do with some good news around here for a change.'

Now it was even more important that I got the part of Pollyanna, not only for myself but for my family so they could finally have something to be pleased about.

The auditions were at nine-thirty in the school hall. Twenty-five of us would be auditioning and we had to do a two-minute improvisation piece in front of the whole class. With improvisation there's no script, so I was going to have to make up everything as I went along.

I was third on, after Wayne Clements whose piece was about a footballer scoring a goal for England in the last minute of the World Cup final. I liked Wayne's piece, even though it did mainly consist of him just shrieking and running up and down.

My piece was about a girl who discovers her cat is dead when she goes to feed it, and I did all

I could to make it as dramatic and as heartbreaking as possible. I got so into it that it felt like I was really holding and speaking to a dead cat not just the air in my hands. Mrs Avery gave me an approving nod when I'd finished. I think she liked it but it was hard to tell.

Nancy was up next, and for her piece she was playing the part of an old lady complaining about her grown-up son not wanting to leave home. It was very funny and she had everyone in stitches.

The last person to audition was Mariella. Her piece was, as she put it, 'Two minutes in the life of a Hollywood It Girl', although as far as I could see it just involved her tottering about the hall like she was some sort of model, giggling and wittering away in a fake American accent. I could hardly understand what she was saying; though it was clear Mrs Avery was enjoying it.

'I'm *so* going to be Pollyanna,' I overheard Mariella say to Alice and Trinity as we all headed back to the classroom. And suddenly I felt very worried.

By the end of the day Mrs Avery was ready to tell us who'd got which part. As she read out the names I found myself feeling more petrified than when I'd been doing my audition.

'The part of Mr Pendleton will be played by Angus O'Leary. The part of Doctor Chilton will be played by Sanjay Kumar. The part of Aunt Polly will be played by Nancy Eyidah.'

'Well done, Nancy,' I whispered to my friend, who looked extremely delighted to get the part she wanted.

If only the same could happen to me, I thought as Mrs Avery read out some more names.

'The part of Jimmy Bean will be played by Wayne Clements; the part of Mrs Snow will be played by Tara Willis. The part of Pollyanna' – an intake of breath shot through the class – 'will be played by Lollyanna Luck.'

Yay! I'd done it! I'd got the part. Nancy gave me a congratulatory hug as Mariella groaned from the desk in front. Unfortunately for her she was going to have to make do with the part of Mrs Tarbell. She gave me a right dirty look, but I couldn't have cared less. I was going to be Pollyanna and that was all that mattered.

My luck was back and was better than ever. At netball practice I scored seven goals in one game, beating a personal best, and my team won twelve–five!

When I got home Mum was sitting in the living

room and I couldn't wait to tell her my good news.

'Mum, you'll never guess what,' I said taking off my coat. 'I got a part in the play. I'm going to be...'

But then I saw her face. It was all blotchy like she'd been crying, and it was obvious she hadn't been listening to me.

'Oh, Lolly,' she reached out her arms.

'Mum, what's wrong?'

'I'm afraid I've got some bad news.'

'What is it?' I asked anxiously as I went over to her.

'No. I'll wait for your father to get back from his, erm...walk. It's probably better we tell you together.' Her voice was trembling.

'Is it Granny Doreen? Has something happened to her?'

'No, she's fine, Lollipop.'

'So what is it then? Please tell me, Mum.'

'It's this place,' she said slowly, her eyes sweeping round the room. She took a deep breath as she cupped my face in her hands. 'I'm afraid we're being repossessed, Lolly. Your father and I fell behind on the mortgage payments and now the bank wants us out. We're going to be homeless, Lollipop.'

Mum's words took a few seconds to sink in. A picture of me, Mum, Dad and Zola sitting beneath a bridge and shivering under a tatty blanket entered my mind.

'Homeless!' I gasped. 'So does that mean we'll be living on the streets, after all?'

My heart thudded as I waited for her response.

'No,' she replied.

Phew.

'The council will have to find us a place. It won't be as nice as this house, mind, but at least we'll have somewhere to live. I'm sorry all this has happened, Lollipop.'

When Zola came home Mum told her what she'd told me. My sister's face went rigid with shock as she tried to take it all in.

'They can't take our house,' she kept saying. 'There must be something we can do to stop them.'

'We did try to reason with the bank, love, explain our situation, that your dad had lost his job but they, erm... They didn't want to know. But we will get through this. We're all just going to have to be strong,' said Mum before gently nudging me. 'We do have some good news, though. Tell her what part you got, Lolly.'

'I'm going to be Pollyanna,' I said, my shoulders

hunched. I should've been feeling ecstatic about it, but Mum's news had put a dampener on my excitement; it was like my birthday all over again.

Zola smiled at me briefly before quickly turning her attention back to Mum. 'What if we staged a sit-in, you know, refused to go; do you think maybe they'd let us stay?'

'Zola, it wouldn't work, trust me,' said Mum. 'I'm so sorry, sweetheart, but there's nothing more we can do apart from accept that this house is no longer ours.'

'Do you think I'm losing my luck?' I asked Zola as I sat on her bed later that evening.

Dad hadn't come back from his walk, which Zola reckoned was because he wanted to keep out of Mum's way. No doubt they'd had an argument before he left.

'People make their own luck, Lolly,' Zola replied. 'It's not something you're born with, you know. It's not a gene in your body.'

'All right, but how come I always win competitions? Explain that. Like today when I got the part of Pollyanna, that was luck, wasn't it?'

'Not quite, Lolly,' said Zola, shaking her head doubtfully. 'You got the part because your teacher thought you were the best person for it.'

I sighed deeply. 'Well, if I was lucky, I think my luck is definitely beginning to disappear. I mean, first Dad loses his job and now we have to leave our home. Everything seems to be going wrong for us.'

Chapter 4

'That's awful,' said Nancy the following evening during our sleepover at her house. I'd just told her my family was going to be homeless. It was such a relief to be able to talk to her about it, since my family were doing their best to avoid even mentioning the subject.

All day my mum and dad had acted as though nothing had happened and instead spoke only about their excitement about me getting the lead part in the play. They even threw me a lunch to celebrate and invited Granny Doreen. Although the lunch was nice it was strange that Granny Doreen had nothing to say about our situation, either. I thought she would've at least made one comment about it seeing as she's so outspoken. She certainly wasn't happy about Dad being unemployed and would make her feelings quite clear on the matter whenever she called or came over.

'You need to find a job, man!' she'd say to Dad in her strong St Lucian accent. 'My Marion can't keep propping up this family. You need to get out dere and search for the work, not waste your time at the computer expecting it to come to you.'

But as we ate Mum's lasagne all Granny Doreen wanted to talk about was her friend Una getting engaged to a man she'd met on a Caribbean cruise. I wasn't interested in hearing about Una, or about the cost of petrol, or the garden hedge, or the butcher's shop that was closing down. I just wanted to know where we were going to live!

I had tried to speak to Zola about it after lunch, but before I could open my mouth it was as if she psychically knew what I was about to say and held up her hand. 'I don't want to talk about it,' she'd said briskly.

'So where will you live?' asked Nancy.

'My dad's going to see the council on Tuesday to see if they have any properties,' I told her.

'Do you reckon you'll have to live far away? Because if you do, you might have to go to a new school,' said Nancy, which immediately had my stomach lurching with worry again.

'I hope not,' I mumbled. 'I'd hate that. We'd never see each other.'

'Promise me you wouldn't forget me,' said Nancy.

'I'd never forget you, Nancy,' I said and put my arm round her. 'You're my bestest friend and if I do have to go to another school then we'll make sure we phone each other every day and have lots of sleepovers.'

'I guess. But I won't be the only one who'd miss you, Lolly, everyone at school will.'

'Everyone except Mariella, you mean. I bet she'd be pleased to see the back of me, especially if it meant her getting the chance to play Pollyanna.' I sighed. 'I suppose I'll just have to keep my fingers crossed that our new house isn't too far away.'

'I'll keep them crossed too,' said Nancy as we held up our fingers.

'They've offered us a flat on the *Landsdale* estate?!' said Mum, her face aghast when Dad announced where the council were planning to house us. 'But it's the roughest estate in the town. No, Austin, there's no *way* we're living there!'

'I'm sorry, Marion, but it was all the accommodation they had. So we either take it or go into some dodgy bed and breakfast.'

'Well I'd rather move in with my mother than live on that estate.'

'Yes, let's live with Granny Doreen, I love her house,' I said.

I didn't want to live on the Landsdale, either. There were always stories in the local newspaper of police raiding it for drugs, or people getting stabbed there.

'We are *not* living with your mother, Marion,' said Dad sharply. 'You know me and her don't see eye to eye. And besides, she's hardly got the space. We'd all be cramped up in that spare room of hers.'

'But, Dad, if we move to the Landsdale, everyone will know that we're poor,' said Zola.

'We are not *poor*,' said Dad fixedly.

But it sure felt like we were.

He then sat down next to Zola. 'Look, sweetheart, we're just a bit down on our luck, that's all, but we'll bounce back, you'll see. And there's no need to worry about the Landsdale, it'll all be fine. The only thing that'll be different is we'll have two bedrooms instead of four.'

'Which means the girls will have to share,' said Mum, sighing. 'Well, at least they won't have to change schools; which seems to be the only good thing about this move.' She looked at me and Zola. 'There's a bus that goes near your schools, which I know for a fact runs past the Landsdale.'

'I think I'd rather change schools than share a room,' declared Zola as she turned to Dad. 'I can't share. I need my own space, Dad.'

'I'm sorry, Zola, but you're going to have to,' he said very bluntly.

'But *none* of my friends have to share a room. God, I hate the place already,' Zola said, tossing up her arms and leaving the room in a sulk.

Mum grimaced. 'And I take it we won't have a garden.'

'Well, we are going to be on the sixth floor, Marion, so I very much doubt it,' said Dad.

'No garden! But where will my trampoline go?' I blurted.

My trampoline was one of the best presents I'd ever got, and even though it was old I loved it.

'I'm sorry, Lollipop, but it looks like we're not going to be able to bring it with us,' Dad admitted.

I felt crushed. My luck was disappearing, fast.

*

The next day was Mrs Avery's last at school. Knowing everyone was feeling sad about it, Mrs Avery did her best to make the day extra special for us. She'd brought in some board games from home and some fancy cakes and crisps for us to eat in the afternoon. I did try to get involved and played two games of Connect Four with Nancy and a game of Hungry Hippos with Angus, but nothing lifted the sad mood I was in, not even a slice of chocolate cake. I just couldn't stop thinking about my family's money problems and having to move to the Landsdale. Would we be safe living there? And would our new flat ever feel like home?

Before the final bell went, we gave Mrs Avery her leaving card. Unfortunately we hadn't done a very good job of it in the end and had made the baby look like some weird alien creature. It had different coloured eyes, one blue and one purple, four nostrils, plus only half of what was supposed to be the left ear (I don't think lazy Ian could be bothered to finish the rest of it) and, although the baby was meant to be a newborn, he not only had a full mane of hair but also a full set of crooked teeth which made him look in urgent need of a dentist. The card was truly hideous. But astonishingly Mrs Avery loved it and was cooing over it as though it was her actual baby come to life.

'He's so cute,' she said, tickling the baby's lopsided chin that was made out of an old yoghurt pot lid. 'You're all such wonderful kids and I know you'll make your new teacher feel very welcome. Thank you again for the card; it's lovely.'

'*I* was the one who came up with the idea to do the baby,' said Mariella, trying to take all the credit.

Oh, shut up! I thought to myself as Mr Kingsley wandered into the classroom. With him was a man who was going to be our supply teacher.

'Hello, everyone, it's nice to meet you. I'm Mr Scott,' he introduced himself. 'Mrs Avery tells me you're a great class so I can't wait to start teaching you. And I'm really looking forward to working with you on your play.' He began looking round the room. 'And which one of you is Lolly?'

I slowly put up my hand. 'Me.'

'Oh, so you're our star?' said Mr Scott, breaking into a big smile. 'Well, I have it on very good authority that you're a fantastic actress so I have no worries that the play will be nothing short of brilliant.'

He looked at Mrs Avery who smiled at me as well and held up two thumbs.

The bell went and it was time for us to say goodbye. As each of us filed out of the class we all let Mrs Avery know how much we'd miss her, and as I passed her desk a part of me felt like begging her not to leave. I didn't want this Mr Scott taking the register or marking my work. He seemed nice, but I didn't want a new teacher, just like I didn't want to move out of my house. I hated all this change.

'I'll miss you, Mrs Avery,' I said to her.

'And I'll miss you too, Lolly. Is everything OK?'

'Yes,' I lied. I wanted to tell her about my family losing our house, but I knew Dad didn't want us talking to people about it, and I didn't want to worry her when she was so happy about her baby.

'Good girl. You take care now and keep on smiling.'

'I will, miss,' I replied, but as I left the room there wasn't a smile on my face, just a great big frown.

A couple of weeks later it was moving week, which was totally exhausting, with cardboard boxes piled up all over the house. Mum took some time off work to pack things up with Dad, and Zola and I had to help out when we got in from school. Auntie

Louise and Mariah came over and helped out a few times too, well, Mariah didn't do anything as she's too little, but she did keep us entertained with her contortionist abilities – fitting her feet into her mouth and lifting her legs way over her head. And she was always laughing, mainly at Dad who kept tripping over things.

'This should be in a box!' he'd fuss, picking up a hairbrush or an old Dora the Explorer doll and waving it at me and Zola.

Dad drove some of the boxes round to Granny Doreen's so she could store them for us. I was hoping she'd be able to take my trampoline, but Dad said it would be too big for her garden so sadly he sold it on eBay along with Mum's exercise machine, a few of his power tools and the garden furniture.

My uncle Finn came down one day from Birmingham and brought an old bunk bed that had belonged to my cousins. It was going to be mine and Zola's now, and as soon as my sister saw it she went into a hissy fit.

'This is *so* humiliating. No one my age sleeps in a bunk bed!' she whined.

But when she saw how stressed Mum looked she didn't mention it again.

It wasn't easy saying goodbye to our old house, and it felt awful seeing it completely empty, my voice echoing as I went from room to room for the final time. Then, as we all walked out of the house, we started to cry. We cried when Dad locked the door for the last time, and we cried when we waved goodbye to the Papathomases as the car turned out of our road, Henley Avenue. But while Mum, Dad and Zola were able to dry their tears, I couldn't stop crying and I cried all the way to our new flat. Zola got a bit cross and kept wrinkling her nose at me, but, unlike her, I'd lived in our old house my whole life. It was all I'd ever known.

'What a dump,' muttered Zola as the car pulled up to the Landsdale, her eyes surveying the four tower blocks that made up the estate.

When we got out of the car she shook her head as she looked at the big lawn in the middle that was littered with old washing machines, a smashed-up TV and a dirty old mattress.

An elderly woman came over to us. She was pushing a buggy that had a black rubbish bag in it instead of a baby.

'Hello. Just moving in?' she asked.

'Yes,' said Mum, flashing the woman a false smile. 'Flat sixty-three.'

'Well, all I can say is don't believe a word you read in the local newspaper. This is a nice estate, but some people would have you believe it's Armageddon round here. There are worse places to live than the Landsdale, I can tell you. Anyway, I hope you enjoy being here. I'm off to the laundrette as my machine's broken down.' She pointed at one of the washing machines on the lawn.

When the removal men took our boxes off their van I quickly discovered that unpacking was a lot worse than packing, and as our new flat was so tiny I felt like a squashed tomato among all our stuff. The flat certainly wasn't as homely as our old house. Mum said it looked like the backdrop of a dreadful seventies film but since I don't think I've seen any dreadful seventies films (I've only seen *Grease* and that was good), I wasn't sure what she meant. Maybe it had something to do with the swirly green wallpaper, which I know she hated because she kept going on about how it was giving her headaches. And she hated the carpet, which I wasn't too fond of, either. It had so many stains in it that it was hard to tell what its original colour was, and in the bathroom it was always squishy and wet. As for my new bedroom, well, it was much, much smaller than my old room. Still, I tried my best to make it feel cosy and put up my paper fans and posters of Corey T.

'Don't tell me I'm going to have to look at his ugly mug every day?' said Zola once I'd finished.

So she put up some posters of her own; one of a cute baby elephant and another of a beach in St Lucia.

At school I didn't tell anyone except Nancy that we'd moved. I didn't want the other children to know in case they'd start seeing me as one of the 'poor kids' – kids who, no matter how nice they were, would always have other people at school taking the mickey out of them. They'd be laughed at for having holes in their clothes or for wearing shoes that never quite fitted, or teased for never coming on school trips or living on rundown estates, just like the Landsdale.

Like me, Zola only told her best friend, Gita, that we'd moved. We didn't want people to even see us near the estate, so every morning we'd catch our bus to school from the high street even though we could've got it from the stop outside the Landsdale.

My mum despised the estate and she continued to argue with Dad, who was spending even more time at the computer.

'You promised to redecorate the flat as soon as we moved in!' she yelled at him one evening.

'I will when I find a job,' he replied. 'Wallpaper isn't cheap, you know.'

'Well, you could've at least tried to clean this place up,' Mum grumbled. 'We've only been here five minutes and already it's looking like a pigsty. What are you doing all day?'

She picked up a dirty cup that had *World's Best Dad* written on it from the coffee table and waved it at him.

'This cup's been here for days. And you need to start putting your papers and CVs away, Austin. We haven't got the space for you to start turning the living room into your own private office. I've been at work all day. Why should I have to come home and start cleaning up after you?'

Then suddenly I found myself in the middle of their argument as Mum turned to me, her hands clasped together. 'Please dream some lottery numbers, Lolly, six winning numbers, so we can move out of this place.'

'I can't *make* the dreams come, Mum, they just happen,' I tried to explain to her.

'I know, sweetheart,' she sighed then gave me a cuddle. 'I'm being silly. I'm still a bit stressed from the move, that's all.'

'We'll come to love this flat, Mum,' I said, trying to be positive.

She smiled weakly. 'If only I could be more like you, Lollipop, always able to see the sunny side of things. You're a good girl and I don't know what we'd do without you,' she said. 'But, yes, hopefully there will come a time when I'm able to love this place.'

However, it didn't take us long to realise that loving the flat would be a lot harder than we'd thought. Well, it wasn't the flat itself that turned out to be the biggest problem, but our noisy neighbours, particularly the ones above us who were always drilling. The sound made me feel like I had a buzzing bee permanently stuck in my ear. The neighbours that lived to the left of us were also very noisy. After a week of living at the Landsdale we still hadn't seen them but, boy, did we hear them! I thought my parents' rows were bad, but they were nothing compared to the shouty arguments the couple next door had. They *SCREEEEEEEEAMED* at each other! I would've loved to have had a garden where I could go and escape the noise. I missed our old garden a lot.

But at least the Landsdale did have some space for me to ride my bike. Sometimes I'd ride it around the estate after school when I'd finished my homework and rehearsed my lines for the play. Mum didn't like me going out by myself, but she was always working overtime these days to bring in some extra money. And Dad was too engrossed in the computer to notice what I was up to.

There were some other kids that played out as well. At first I was worried that they'd be horrible to me, seeing as some of them looked quite scary, even the little, little kids. But they all turned out to be really friendly, and sometimes we'd all play tag outside my block.

But I wish I hadn't played tag with them one Thursday afternoon. I was 'It' and was chasing a boy called Aiden, when suddenly on the other side of the road I spotted Trinity from school. She was standing outside a house with her mum and dad and was hugging an old woman. Straightaway I wanted to run off so she didn't see me, but it was too late, she already had. And as the sneaky grin popped up on Trinity's face I knew that my secret of living on the Landsdale wasn't going to be a secret for long.

Chapter 5

I was really worried that Trinity would go blabbing straight away to everyone that she'd seen me on the Landsdale and, as I rode the bus to school the next day, I tried to think of all the excuses I could use for being there. I could say that I was visiting a sick aunt, perhaps, or that I was out jogging in the neighbourhood. But I knew none of my excuses sounded at all believable.

'Trinity saw me playing outside my new flat yesterday,' I told Nancy as soon as I got to school. 'She knows where I live now, and I bet you she'll tell Mariella, and then everyone will know. They're going to call me names, Nancy. They're going to know we've lost our house and all our money – and they're going to make my life hell.'

'No they won't and, anyway, it's none of their business where you live. Just because you live on the Landsdale it doesn't make you a bad person. And if anyone does call you names, Lolly, well, they're being bullies and we'll tell Mr Kingsley.'

We linked arms and wandered round the playground.

'So what's it like sharing a room with Zola?' she asked.

'*Annoying*,' I groaned. 'She snores like a rhino and when I tell her about it she always makes out that she doesn't snore at all.'

'Oh, Lolly Luck!' a voice called.

We turned round and standing behind us were Trinity and Mariella.

'What do you want?' I asked. But I knew exactly what they wanted. It was written all over their sneering faces.

'I hear you're living on the Landsdale,' said Mariella, her voice all snide.

I tried not to look bothered. 'So?' I answered.

Mariella smirked and twirled a finger around a lock of her curly black hair.

'That estate's well grotty. My gran hates living opposite it,' said Trinity.

'My mum says it's a no-go area full of drug addicts and murderers,' added Mariella. 'And apparently the whole place is infested with fleas.'

She suddenly took a step back pulling Trinity with her. 'Don't stand too close, Trin. You might catch something!'

Trinity shuddered and pretended to scratch her arms.

'So what happened to your house? Your parents lose all their money?' Mariella asked, giving me a false sympathetic look.

I stared at her icily. 'No.'

'They must have, otherwise you wouldn't be living in that flea pit and you wouldn't be looking so scruffy. Your shirt looks like it hasn't been washed in years.'

'*Urgh*, gross,' mocked Trinity.

'Not that it's any of your business but my shirt was washed the other night, if you'd like to know,' I replied stoutly even though it wasn't actually true. To save on electricity we were now using the washing machine only once a week, and since Mum didn't add my shirt to the last big wash she'd done I'd been wearing it now for two whole weeks.

A crowd had started gathering around us, kids from all years, some jeering and whispering, waiting for a fight.

Mariella started laughing. 'Watch out, everyone. Lolly's got fleas. That's what happens if you live on the Landsdale.'

'Do you want a punch, Mariella? Because I'd be very happy to give you one right now,' I retorted as the jeering got louder.

Mariella blinked, and for a moment she looked worried, but then her lips curled up into a cruel smile.

'Want to punch me do you, Lolly?' she challenged, her voice turning shrill. 'I'm not scared of you. And it's not as if you've got Zola here, so I can say what I want.'

I tilted my head to the side as a chorus of 'Fight, fight, fight!' broke out among the crowd.

'I don't need my sister to look out for me. I can deal with you all by myself,' I replied, raising my arm quickly and slinging it Mariella's way. But someone grabbed hold of it before I could reach her. It was Mr Scott.

'What on earth are you doing?' he asked, putting my arm down.

'Sir, Lolly, she was . . . she was going to hit me,' said Mariella and burst into tears – all fake, of course.

'She was making fun of me, sir,' I said.

'Yes that's right, Mr Scott, she was making fun of Lolly,' said Nancy.

'No I wasn't, sir,' whimpered Mariella looking at me slyly. 'It's Lolly's who's been . . . bullying me.'

'No I haven't,' I said, disgusted at her evil lie. I looked up at Mr Scott, my eyes pleading with him to believe me. 'I'm not a bully.'

Although Mr Scott didn't say it, I think he did believe me. But I still had to go and see Mr Kingsley, who gave me a long telling off for my 'threatening behaviour'. Plus, I was going to have to spend three lunch times in detention as punishment. Mariella Sneddon was now my arch, arch-enemy. I disliked her more than ever.

'Guess what?' said Dad when I got in from school.

'What?'

'I've got an interview,' he exclaimed, lifting me up and spinning me round. 'It's next Wednesday. I can't believe it; I've actually got an interview, Lollipop!'

'That's excellent, Dad.'

'I'm so chuffed,' he said. 'It's the most brilliant news I've had in months.'

Mum was chuffed too and swooped a hand

across her forehead when Dad told her the good news.

'Finally!' she said and gave him a hug. 'I'm pleased for you, love, really I am.'

The next few days were a whirl of excitement as all of us helped Dad prepare for his interview. Zola and I helped him choose the suit he was going to wear while Mum helped him practise his interview techniques by pretending to be the person interviewing him.

Getting a job interview had really made a difference to Dad. He'd become a lot happier, and he and Mum were getting on like they used to. They didn't argue once and Dad even started to help Mum around the flat, tidying up and washing the dishes.

To celebrate getting an interview, Dad decided to take us all out for dinner. I'd never been to an all-you-can-eat Chinese buffet before, and seeing so much food made me feel a little giddy. Everything looked scrummy-scrum-scrumptious and I copied Zola in cramming as much of it as I could onto my plate. When I got back to our table my plate looked like a weird towering sculpture with food pointing out at all angles. There was lemon chicken and satay chicken, pork balls and prawn balls, crispy duck and crispy seaweed, spring rolls that were cylindrical and spring rolls that were triangular, beef foo yung and special foo yung, Singapore fried rice and egg fried rice, broccoli in black-bean sauce and mushrooms in oyster sauce, banana fritters and lots and lots of chips. I stuck my fork in and got started. *Delicious*.

'The banana fritter really goes well with the lemon chicken,' I told everyone.

'*Urgh!*' Zola recoiled. 'You're not meant to put the dessert on the same plate as the mains.'

'So I was thinking,' said Dad to Mum, 'that if I get the job we can start looking at finding somewhere else to live.'

Mum nodded. 'Perhaps we could rent a house back near our old place. I miss that neighbourhood so much.'

'And will the house have a garden?' I asked.

Dad grinned. 'Yes, Lollipop, we'll make sure the house has a garden.'

He looked at Mum. 'I have a good feeling about this interview, Marion. I know they say you shouldn't count your chickens before they hatch, but I think I'm going to get this job.'

'Why, Dad?' I asked.

'Do you remember my friend Jake? Well, he

works for this company now, and he knows the man who'd be my manager really well. He's put in a good word for me. He says I'm just the sort of person they're looking for.'

'I hope you get it,' said Mum touching his hand. 'And thanks for taking us out tonight, Austin. It's been nice to sit down and have dinner as a family.'

Dad kissed Mum on the lips. 'Thanks, Marion. I know things have been hard, but we're turning a corner now. Look, let's not worry about money tonight. I think we both deserve a special treat.'

He called over a waitress. 'A bottle of champagne, please,' he said and winked at Mum.

I smiled. It felt really good seeing my parents so happy and loved-up again.

It was a relief to get back home from the restaurant, though. I was so tired, and absolutely stuffed from all the food I'd eaten. Mum had drunk too much champagne so Dad had to practically carry her up six flights of stairs as the lifts were out of order. When we got in, he plopped her down on the sofa, but she couldn't stay upright and was leaning to one side, a big clownish grin on her face. I'd never seen my mum drunk before; it was funny and embarrassing and a bit scary all at the same time.

'Girls, keep an eye on your mother. I'm just going to check if we've had any messages,' said Dad walking over to the telephone.

'I don't need anyone keeping an eye on me,' babbled Mum. Then she started giggling, 'I'm a grown woman; I can keep an eye on myself, two eyes, in fact, or three eyes – if I had three eyes.'

Zola switched on the TV, flicking it onto an American police drama, which had Mum bolting upright and pointing at the screen with excitement. 'Ooh, look at him! He's so handsome. Reminds me of your dad when we first met.'

'No,' said Dad suddenly. At first I thought he was talking about the actor on TV, but when I asked him what he meant he just looked at me completely dazed. 'I . . . um . . . I . . . don't have an interview any more,' he said very slowly.

'How come?' asked Zola.

'There was a message . . . from Jake. He said the person that's in the job . . . they've, um . . . changed their mind about leaving and the company are happy for them to stay on. They've withdrawn the vacancy.'

'Don't worry, Dad, there'll be other interviews,' I said and joined Zola in giving him a hug.

'There was I thinking some luck was finally coming my way,' he murmured. 'Maybe I was just born to be *un*lucky.'

He looked like he was about to cry as Mum started clapping her hands.

'Give the man a round of applause, why don't you? Austin Luck makes a mess of things once again.'

She wobbled up onto her feet. *'I've got a good feeling about this one*,' she mocked in a whiney high-pitched voice. '*Things will change, Marion*. Ha! And to think I believed you. My father said you'd end up disappointing me. He always thought you were a waste of space. Well, maybe I should have listened to him, cos nothing's going to change, is it? We're going to be stuck in this hellhole for ever!'

'Don't start, Marion, not when we've had such a good evening. I really can't cope with any more grief right now.'

'Grief?' said Mum, her eyes widening with rage.

'Here we go again,' whispered Zola in my ear. 'I'm not sticking around to listen to this, I'm going to bed.'

'Let me tell *you* something about grief, Mr Luck,' said Mum as Zola flounced off to our bedroom. 'Grief is having the home you so dearly loved taken away from you. Grief is wondering whether your electricity will be cut off and you'll be reduced to feeling your way around in the dark. And grief is not being able to afford a joint of beef from the supermarket for the Sunday roast and instead having to make do with tuna pasta again and again and again!'

I didn't mind tuna pasta but, truthfully, I did miss our Sunday roasts.

'So, Austin, what next? What are you going to do?' yelled Mum as she walked tipsily round the sofa.

'I'll keep looking – that's all I can do,' Dad shrugged.

'Which means you'll be out of work yet another month. And, of course, it'll be me who'll have to keep this family going.'

'He *will* find a job, Mum,' I said, feeling annoyed by how horrible she was being to Dad. Couldn't she see he was as disappointed as she was?

She snorted. 'Maybe your father wouldn't be in this situation if he'd gone for that supermarket job when I told him to. But oh no, Austin, you were too much of a snob to apply.'

'Just stop, Marion,' said Dad, sitting down in his recliner. 'You're drunk and you're embarrassing yourself.'

He looked over at me. 'Lolly, I think it's time you went to bed.'

I nodded. That was fine by me. Like Zola, I didn't fancy being around another argument.

'Why did Mum have to spoil a lovely evening?' said Zola as I came into our bedroom. She was lying on her bed in the dark with all her clothes still on. 'I wish I was old enough to move out.'

I blinked at her. 'You don't mean that, do you?' I said, switching on the bedside lamp.

'*Don't you dare mention my girls!*' we heard Mum scream.

'I do mean it,' said Zola. 'I hate this flat, I hate this estate and I hate Mum and Dad quarrelling all the time. I want our old life back.'

'*It's not as if* you've *been looking after them these past few months, putting food in their mouths and paying their bus fares. No. All you've done is sit on your big backside doing nothing. I lost my beautiful house because of you.*'

'I've had enough of this,' huffed Zola, climbing down from her bunk and going over to our CD shelf. She looked through the CDs. 'I know I'm not a really fan but do you fancy listening to some Corey T?' she asked.

'Cool. Thanks, Zola,' I said.

We listened to a whole album turned up loud, but still the argument continued in the next room. Zola kept turning up the stereo because Mum and Dad were saying some really awful stuff to each other and we didn't want to hear it. Then it would go quiet and we'd think that they'd stopped so we'd turn the music down, but it was like they'd just been getting their breath back. Before we knew it, it had all started up again. And on and on it went. They'd had big rows before, of course, but this one was definitely the worst. I knew it was probably because Mum was a bit drunk, but still, they were saying things that I knew would really hurt and they'd have trouble forgetting.

And then it happened – the horrendous moment when my whole life changed for ever. The moment I'll never forget as long as I live.

'*For the last time, I am not a failure!*' Dad's voice boomed through the paper-thin wall. '*Stop talking about YOUR girls. They're my kids as well, and I'm trying to do my best for them!*'

'No, *they're my kids, Austin, mine! Lolly's not even yours, for pity's sake! You're not her real dad.*'

I gasped. It was as if a bomb had gone off in the flat and all the air had been sucked from my lungs. I felt like I couldn't breathe. The blood started pounding in my ears and I actually thought I might be sick. I heard Zola gasp in the bed above me and I knew she was lying there, her mouth open wide; her face as horrified as mine.

'*What did you say?*' said Dad. Or was it me? I couldn't tell.

It had all gone quiet on the other side of the door, but Mum's words stayed with me, echoing around and around my head. And, even though I was lying as still as a mouse, I felt like I was spinning and the whole room was spinning with me.

'*The girls – do you think they heard?*' asked Mum, trying to whisper – but we could hear everything.

Zola climbed off her bed and onto mine. 'Mum's drunk, Lolly. It's not true what she said, it's not true,' she kept repeating, holding her arms tight around me.

'Yes, you're right. It can't be true,' I wanted to say back. But I couldn't speak; my words tangled up in my throat like a ball of wool.

'*Is she or isn't she my daughter?*' Dad's voice suddenly blared.

Then it went silent again.

'*No, Marion, nooooooooooooo,*' we heard him howl.

And it was like everything was going in slow motion – Zola, stroking my hair, telling me not to be scared, not to get upset. But although she was there with her arms around me, I'd never felt so alone.

'*Oh my God, oh my God!*' Dad started to wail over and over, quietly then loudly, quickly then slowly, so that it almost sounded like he was singing a song. '*This can't be happening. Who is he? Who's her father?*'

Silence.

'*ANSWER ME, WOMAN!*'

'*Quincy*,' we heard Mum say. My mind was too muddled up to try and figure out who Quincy was.

'*What? Who you used to work with . . . ?*' Dad blustered after a short while, '*He's Lolly's real father?*'

'*Keep your voice down, Austin, please,*' Mum begged him.

'*How could you do this to me, Marion, lie to me about my little girl . . . ?*' Dad let his voice trail away.

After a few minutes the shouting stopped and then came a knock on the door. Zola and I looked towards it, but didn't answer. We just lay there, huddled together. The person knocked again but then went away.

I started to cry, my whole body shaking with tears.

'Don't cry, Lolly,' said my sister, drying my face with her hands.

But she was unable to fight the tears herself, the two of us bawled our eyes out.

Chapter 6

It took me ages to get to sleep. I just couldn't switch my mind off. I kept trying to make sense of what I'd heard. Only nothing made sense. How could Dad not be my dad? People were always saying how much I looked like him, how I had his nose and the same heart-shaped face. So how could someone else be my dad, some total stranger? I was meant to be the luckiest member of the Luck family. But did this mean I wasn't a Luck at all?

It was like last night had been a terrible dream and for a moment when I woke up the next day I thought that it had been. As I opened my eyes I thought I was waking up in my old bed in our old house, but then Zola snored from the bunk above, the neighbour upstairs started drilling, and bins crashed and banged outside, reminding me that I wasn't in my old bed in our old house, but in my poky new room in our poky new flat and today was dustbin day.

I crept out of the bedroom and made my way to the kitchen. Dad was asleep in the living room when I passed, still wearing his jeans and shirt from last night, and when I went into the kitchen Mum was there staring into space. She jumped when she saw me.

'Lolly. I didn't hear you come in.' She looked exhausted. 'Would you like some breakfast?'

I wasn't hungry. My stomach was still churning. I wanted to ask her why she'd lied to me, lied to all of us, but I couldn't seem to put my thoughts into a question. The words scattered about in my head like a game of Scrabble.

I shrugged.

'I know what, I'll get you some cornflakes,' she said.

She opened one of cupboards and took out the box of cereal then went over to the fridge to fetch some milk. She kept glancing at me, and I knew that she knew I'd heard what she'd said about Dad not being my dad. I'd never felt more angry with her. I tried to go back to my room, but she put her arm round me and guided me to the table.

'Come and sit down, love,' she said, her voice wobbling. 'I'm guessing you probably heard a bit of what was said last night and I can't begin to imagine what you must be feeling...'

I didn't answer her, nor did I sit down.

'I'm so sorry, Lollipop. I never said what I did to hurt you or your dad. It slipped out and that's unforgiveable of me. There are no excuses for what I've done.'

'So it's true,' I said, looking at her coldly. 'You had an affair, or something? Dad's not my real dad?'

She paused then slowly nodded her head, tears rolling down her cheeks. 'Well, he's not your biological father, no, but he loves you like you're his own and he always will. He adores you, Lolly. And that will never change.'

But I didn't want to hear that. I wanted proper answers.

'So who is my real dad?'

'I know it must have come as a great shock and it'll probably take you a while to come to terms with it all,' she muttered, putting my bowl of cornflakes onto the kitchen table. 'You didn't deserve to find out like that. I'm such an idiot.'

'Who's my dad, Mum?' I pressed.

'Please sit down, sweetheart.'

'I don't want to sit down!'

'OK, OK.' She paused. 'Your father is my old manager. He left the company some years back. His name's Quincy. Quincy Knight.'

I swallowed hard as I let it sink in.

'And does he know about me?'

'Yes,' she murmured, but then quickly changed the subject. 'I don't think I'll go into the office today. I do have lots to do, though, so I'll probably just work from home.'

'I'm not going to school,' I said stiffly.

'Lollipop, you have to go to school,' said Mum, putting her head to one side.

She shuffled towards me, her arms outstretched. 'Come here, sweetheart. Let me give you a hug. It won't make up for what I've done, but I want you to know that I love you so much.'

I took a step back. I didn't want her anywhere near me in case all my angry feelings came out at once in a bite, kick, punch, scratch. I felt like hurting her like she'd hurt me.

'No!' I yelled and ran off to the bathroom locking the door behind me.

I flopped down onto the toilet seat and ripped off a sheet of loo roll to make a paper fan. It didn't look as good as the fans I make out of proper paper, but it did sort of help me to calm down. I made another one, concentrating hard as I folded forward, folded backwards, folded forward, folded backwards, folded forward, folded backwards...

Dad knocked on the door. 'Lolly, are you all right?'

But I didn't say anything. I didn't want to see him. I didn't want to see if he'd changed towards me, if he'd stopped loving me.

Then Mum knocked. 'Please, sweetheart, please open the door.'

'Go away!'

'But we're worried about you, Lolly. Please come out.'

My hand hovered over the lock, then I heard movement outside in the hallway and the front door slammed. And I knew it was Dad who'd gone out.

'Lolly,' Mum said. 'Come out, love.'

'I don't want to!'

'But I want to talk to you, Lollipop.'

'I hate you, Mum. *I hate you!*' I screamed.

She immediately went quiet, then after about a

minute she spoke again. 'I don't blame you for hating me, Lolly, I don't blame any of you. I did a bad thing, which I regret. But I've never regretted having you, and the reason I didn't tell you the truth sooner was because I was trying to protect you. All of you. I wanted to make this family work.'

I unlocked the door.

'I put some raspberries on your cornflakes,' said Mum, holding out the bowl and acting as if everything was back to normal. As if a few raspberries could fix things.

I barged past her and went straight to my bedroom. She called my name, but didn't follow.

Zola was awake, her head poking out from under the duvet like a meerkat checking to see if it was safe to emerge.

'Did last night really happen?'

'Yeah, it happened, all right,' I replied miserably.

'I can't believe you're not my sister, I mean that you're my half…' Zola's voice petered out.

'I can't believe it, either.'

'I'm scared, Lolly. What if Mum and Dad get divorced?'

I climbed up to her bed and handed her one of my toilet-paper fans.

'Oh, you and your dumb fans,' she said, but she smiled at me kindly.

'I was just trying to make you feel better.'

'I think it's going to take a lot more than a fan to cheer everyone up this time, Lolly. Mum and Dad are probably going to split up now. I know it was all a long time ago, but she did cheat on him. And he might not be able to forgive her for that.'

'No! They can't split up, Zola. They love each other really,' I said, clutching hold of my sister's hand. As angry as I was with Mum, I certainly didn't want her and Dad to get divorced. 'They can't split up, they just can't!'

Chapter 7

I really couldn't concentrate at school and the morning felt like a big blur full of boring maths sums and a boring presentation about gravity. I hardly said anything to Nancy, which had her really worried.

'Are you all right, Lolly?' she asked me at lunch time. 'Has something happened?'

'No, nothing's happened. I'm fine,' I insisted and put on my brightest smile, but inside I couldn't have been more devastated.

There was a rehearsal for the play after lunch and, even though I was pleased that we had one, I was scared that my acting would be terrible. To my surprise, though, I was brilliant, so brilliant, in fact, that I had Mr Scott in tears, which was quite a shock as he never struck me as the crying kind. But, then again, the scene was one of the more emotional ones. It was where Aunt Polly tells Pollyanna that she won't be able to walk again and Pollyanna is distraught. But all the crying I did was real – I'd put all the hurt I was feeling into that moment. Mr Scott said my performance was outstanding and that he could imagine me becoming a film star one day. Some of the kids wanted to know if I'd sneaked in a couple onions to bring on the tears. I told them no, but they rolled their eyes disbelievingly.

I stayed on after school for netball practice, which was a huge mistake as I played abysmally and kept giving possession of the ball to Mariella. My team ended up losing the game, which, of course, meant Mariella had a smug grin on her face. I felt really bad that I'd made my team lose, and when we got back to the changing room I broke down in tears in front of everyone.

All the girls and Miss Jennings, our PE teacher, were milling around me wanting to know what was wrong, but I didn't want to talk to them. I didn't know what to say. They were all very concerned, except for Mariella, who kept looking at Trinity and pretending to yawn.

'Nancy, why don't you stay with her? Maybe you'll be able to find out what's the matter,' said Miss Jennings before hurrying the others out.

'Lolly, please tell me what's upsetting you,' my friend whispered as she sat down next to me. 'I know something's wrong. You've been quiet all day. Is it something really bad?'

I nodded as I took a deep breath and slowly told Nancy about last night. And when I finished speaking it was like she hadn't a clue of what to say back, her face completely dumbstruck. 'So your real dad,' she eventually muttered, 'is your Mum's ex-boss!'

I nodded solemnly.

Nancy blinked. 'So that means your mum had an affair. Omigod!'

'My real dad, he's called Quincy Knight. I don't know where he lives or if he even has other children... but I don't care about him. It's not as if he's ever been interested in knowing me, otherwise he would've got in touch.' I grimaced. 'I wish things could go back to how they were before my birthday when Dad lost his job. Everything was perfect then, and we were all so happy.'

'But maybe it's a good thing that you know the truth. I mean, you wouldn't want to go through your whole life thinking a man was your dad when he wasn't,' said Nancy. 'You might not have found out the truth until you were an old lady, Lolly.'

'But knowing the truth just makes me feel sad,' I replied, bowing my head. 'I feel like I'm in a nightmare and I can't wake up.'

'Do you think your parents will get a divorce?' asked Nancy.

'I don't want them to, but Zola reckons they will.'

'Well if they do, you'll survive it, Lolly, just like I did,' she said reassuringly. 'And what about your real dad, do you want to meet him?'

'I don't know. My mind's too muddled up right now—' I said and paused. 'I should've worked it out, Nancy, you know, that I wasn't my dad's daughter.'

'But how could you have known?'

'Well, when I think about it, me and Zola, we've never looked like proper sisters. Her nose is different from mine and she has a big forehead and I don't, or do I?'

'No, you've got a small forehead,' said Nancy.

'And I'm the only one in my family who's lucky,

well used to be lucky. No one else ever won anything, which means I must've got my luck from my real dad, Quincy. But I don't want him to be my dad, Nancy. Why couldn't he have just left my mum alone? She was happy with Dad before *he* came along. It's all his fault, you know, all of this, and it'll be his fault if my mum and dad get divorced.'

I looked up at Nancy. 'No, I don't want to meet him, not ever. I hate him, Nancy. I hate him!'

Nancy's mum gave me a lift home and when I got in Mum, Zola, Auntie Louise, Mariah and Granny Doreen were all sitting around Dad who was standing in the middle of the room, a holdall bag beside his feet.

'Dad!' I blurted. 'What's going on?'

He turned round to look at me, his face desperately sad. 'I'm sorry, Lolly, but I have to . . .'

'Have to what?' I said. But I already knew the answer. He was leaving us.

'Please don't go, Austin,' Mum pleaded with him. 'We need you.'

'I have to go, Marion. You had a child with another man. How can I stay?' he replied. 'And you not only lied about Lolly, but you lied about Great-Uncle Ernest.'

'Great-Uncle Ernest?' I said fretfully as Granny Doreen came over to me. 'What's happened to him?'

'Let's go to the kitchen, Lolly,' she said, taking hold of my hand. 'You shouldn't be listening to dis grown-up talk. I'll fix you someting to eat.'

'I don't want anything to eat. I want to know what's happened to Great-Uncle Ernest.'

'I'm afraid he doesn't exist, Lolly, that's what's happened,' said Dad.

I swallowed hard and blinked at him in confusion. 'I don't understand. What do you mean he doesn't exist?'

'It seems your mother made him up to hide the fact that it was Quincy who'd been sending you money all this time. I guess I was just an idiot for not working it out sooner. Your mother only started speaking of a great-uncle Ernest after you were born. It certainly makes sense now why he'd send birthday cards to you and not Zola.'

I couldn't believe it. *Great-Uncle Ernest was really my dad!* My body quivered with shock. I suddenly felt dizzy and stumbled backwards into Gran's arms.

'Cha, Austin! Dere was no need to tell her,' said Granny Doreen, sucking her teeth and straightening me up. 'Now Lolly's all distressed.'

'Oh, go suck on a bonbon, Doreen!' scoffed Dad. 'You're nothing but a big hypocrite. You knew all along Marion was lying and yet you chose to keep quiet, you and Louise.'

Auntie Louise and Granny Doreen knew! It was like someone had punched me in the stomach.

'Me sorry,' was all Granny Doreen could mutter as I looked up at her, bewildered, the wrinkles on her face creasing with pity as she sat me down on the sofa, the snack in the kitchen forgotten.

'Austin, I know what my Marion did was wrong,' said Granny Doreen to Dad, her voice softening, 'but it did happen a long time ago. And look what came out of it – a wonderful, beautiful child who I know you love with all your heart. So, please, tink carefully about what you're doing.'

'I do love Lolly,' muttered Dad looking towards me, his lips pulled back in a half-frown, half-smile. 'She's my precious little girl . . . but it feels like my heart's been ripped right out . . . And I don't know what to think or feel any more. I have to get away. I need space to get my head together.'

'I'm sorry, Austin,' said Mum, getting up suddenly and grabbing hold of Dad's arm. 'I know it'll probably take a while, but I'm begging you, please forgive me.'

'You made me swear when we got married that we wouldn't keep secrets from each other, and there you've been keeping the biggest secret of them all!' Dad boomed, wriggling his arm free from Mum.

'I'm a fool, I know that, but please, Austin, don't spite the girls. They need you as much as I do. They'll be heartbroken if you leave.'

Dad picked up his bag.

'Please don't go!' cried Zola.

I wanted to say the same thing, but all I could do was look on helplessly.

'Take care, girls,' said Dad, giving me and Zola a limp wave.

I burst into tears immediately.

'See, the girls don't want you to go, either,' sobbed Mum.

Dad said nothing as he headed out into the hall and straight for the door, but Mum beat him to it, refusing to let him pass.

'Get out of my way, Marion,' he said steadily, but there was no mistaking the resentment in his voice.

She shook her head. 'No, I'm not letting you go!'

'Oi! I'll call the police if you don't blimmin' shut up!' a voice yelled through the wall. I think it was the noisy man next door. He was banging too but Mum took no notice.

'Please, Austin, please don't leave us!' she shrieked.

'Use your brain, Austin! Can't you see that my sister loves you,' said Auntie Louise as she cradled Mariah, who was screaming her little head off.

'I *am* using my brain, Louise,' said Dad. 'And it's telling me to get the hell out of here. Goodbye.'

He shoved Mum to the side, opened the door and walked out.

'Talk to me, Austin, please!' said Mum, running after him.

Zola wanted to run after him too, but Granny Doreen stopped her in her tracks.

'Stay inside, Zola. Your parents need to sort this out by dem selves.'

I quickly went into the kitchen and peered through the window. Dad came out first, with Mum scuttling behind, her slippers clopping against the concrete. He ran over to where our car was and quickly got in.

'Don't do this!' I could hear Mum shouting as she banged on the windows.

But it was too late – Dad had started the ignition and was driving off. Mum tried to give chase, but she couldn't catch him. My dad was gone.

Chapter 8

We stayed up really late that night, Mum, Zola and me, waiting for Dad, hoping he'd just gone to the pub 'to drown his sorrows' as Granny Doreen put it before returning home. Only he didn't come home, not that night, or the next night, or the night after that. He didn't phone to tell us where he was, and when we called his mobile it just kept going straight to voicemail. We left him heaps of messages, but it was like he'd disappeared off the face of the earth. No one had seen him, not his brother, Uncle Finn, or the rest of the family, or any of his friends. Mum was crying so much that her eyes were constantly red from all the tears that had been spurting out.

Seeing my mum so sad made me not feel as angry with her. I even made her a couple of paper fans to cheer her up and got her to help me practise my lines for the play. I think it helped a little bit, but I'd still hear her crying in her bedroom late at night.

I was crying a lot myself because I was really missing Dad and finding it hard to get my head around the fact that I wasn't his daughter. I started to become really clumsy too, dropping and knocking stuff over by accident. It was like all the stress in my mind had gone down into my hands and legs turning me into a total klutz. I broke at least two plates and a couple of glasses. I also broke a very expensive crystal vase that Dad had bought Mum for her fortieth birthday. She tried to pretend that it didn't matter, but I knew she was really hurt that I'd broken it. I broke something of Nancy's too; a brand-new Hello Kitty watch that her dad had got her. She'd taken it off her wrist to show me but I wasn't quite holding it properly and it dropped to the ground with a clunk. It didn't look broken at first, but when Nancy picked it up it wasn't ticking. Thankfully she wasn't cross with me and she even gave me a nice hug when I started crying and told her how much I was missing my dad.

The Easter holidays soon arrived, but we still hadn't heard from Dad. It felt really strange not seeing him or hearing his voice, especially on Easter Sunday when normally he and Mum would give us our Easter eggs together but instead it was just Mum who gave us our eggs. And usually it was Dad who'd carve the roast lamb for Easter lunch, but this year it was Granny Doreen doing the carving. She'd also done the cooking as Mum was too upset to do it herself, but none of us really enjoyed the meal even though it was the first proper Sunday roast we'd had in ages.

Granny Doreen stayed with us for a couple of days after that, helping Mum out around the flat. She made us lots of other nice meals, including her delicious green-fig and saltfish pie, but unfortunately I could only eat tiny amounts, my stomach feeling constantly queasy. Mum and Zola seemed to have the same tummy trouble as well as they too ate very little.

'You girls have to eat. It's not right dat man is putting you off your food,' remarked Granny Doreen one evening.

'"That man" you're referring to is my husband, Mum, and we all miss him terribly,' my mum replied.

'But he's probably at some friend's house,' said Granny Doreen. 'And me bet you *he's* not going hungry.'

'He can't be at a friend's house because nobody's seen him, Mum.'

'Marion, he's fine. I doubt his body is lying in a ditch somewhere so will you please stop worrying,' said Granny Doreen, trying to be helpful but being very *unhelpful*.

We hadn't considered that Dad might be dead until then. Zola got really upset and begged Mum to call the police and report Dad as missing. But Granny Doreen managed to talk her out of it, convincing Mum that Dad was alive and all we needed to do was wait for him to get in touch. Still, this didn't stop us from fretting, which really annoyed Granny Doreen.

'Thank goodness me going home tonight,' she said to us on her final day at the flat. 'Since me get here you girls have done nothing but mope about. It's like being at a funeral. I don't tink I see any of you smile once. Tell me someting, you forget how to smile?' She waggled her head at us. 'You know, when I was a child in St Lucia my mudda always told me to put on a smile no matter how tough tings were. She'd say, "Doreen, girl, a smile is like medicine. It fill us with joy, fill us with hope".'

'But what do we have to smile about?' my mum asked grimly.

'A lot, Marion! Whether it's the air in your lungs or the birds chirping in the sky,' said Granny Doreen. 'Look, me know Austin not here, but that don't mean your lives have to stop. So, as this is my last day, I was tinking we should go out, do someting fun. My treat.'

So, that Saturday, at Gran's insistence, we all put on our best clothes before getting into a cab to take us to our first stop on her 'Fantastically Fun Tour' – a luxurious hotel for afternoon tea. The tea was very, very nice, and the sandwiches were just as I liked them, with all the crusts cut off. But it was the chocolate éclairs that I loved the most – they were *amaazzzing*. Mum almost choked on her éclair when the bill arrived even though she knew she wouldn't be paying for it. But Granny Doreen didn't seem too bothered as she pulled out her pink credit card.

The next stop on her 'Fantastically Fun Tour' was a beauty spa. It was my first time at a spa and I was hoping I'd get to have lots of treatments done, but Granny Doreen said that Zola and I didn't need them as we were 'beautiful already' so she only let us have a manicure, which was fine, I guess. Zola got her nails covered in this sparkly pink polish and I had yellow polish put on, which made my nails look ultra lush. Mum came out of her aromatic body massage looking really relaxed and smelling like a bunch of flowers. Gran had got herself a facial and was grinning from ear to ear when the spa manager told her how it made her look more like Mum's sister than her mother.

Our final stop on Granny Doreen's tour was the cinema, where we went and watched a romantic-comedy film. It was really funny, but it did have a bit of a weepy ending, which had Mum crying bucket loads.

Gran had her arm round her as we walked out and was whispering something to her. I couldn't make out what she was saying, but when we got into the foyer it was Gran who was the one looking sad.

'Me shouldn't have taken you to see that film. It was a bad idea,' she said, sighing heavily.

'No, today's been brilliant,' my mum said. 'I'm just feeling a bit emotional, but I did enjoy the movie – and all of the other things we've done today. So thank you, Mum.'

'Yes, thanks, Gran. Today has been fantastically fantastic,' I said enthusiastically.

'I want to see *that* film when it comes out,' said Zola, pointing at a poster of her favourite actor, Brendan Rush, on the wall.

'We should all go and see it when it's released,' said Mum as we stepped onto the escalator.

'Looks like the next showing is going to be popular,' remarked Granny Doreen, staring down at the entrance. 'Just look at all dem people coming in.'

I looked too. Then suddenly my heart began to thump.

'D-d-d—' I couldn't even say his name as I zipped past Gran and ran down the rest of the escalator.

'Lolly, where are you going? Come back here!' Mum shouted after me. But I wasn't going to lose him, not again.

I quickly raced towards the people queuing for tickets as I searched for him.

'Dad, Dad!' I yelled, weaving my way through the crowd and hoping he could hear me. 'Dad!'

Then I spotted him over at the ice-cream counter. I bolted towards him, flinging my arms around his waist.

'I'm so glad I saw you, Dad. I've missed you

so much,' I sobbed with delight. But Dad was trying to wriggle away from me.

'Please get off me!'

'Huh?' I murmured as I looked up at Dad – only it wasn't my dad but some random man who happened to look like him.

I gasped and immediately stepped back.

'I'm sorry, little girl, but I'm not your father,' said the man, looking spooked.

A woman came over, waving tickets. 'What is it, Patrick?' she asked, glancing at him then at me.

'This little girl thinks I'm her dad,' he said, his lips stretched sideways.

'Oh, no, have you lost your dad?' said the woman, crouching down and looking at me sadly.

I was shaking. I started to speak but more tears began springing from my eyes and I was wailing like a baby.

'Oh, you poor thing,' the woman exclaimed as I turned my head away from her.

Then Mum found me. 'Why did you run off like that, Lolly?' she asked, sounding cross. But her voice softened when she saw my tears. 'Oh, sweetheart, whatever is the matter?'

'I thought it was him, Mum,' I said, my voice rattling and thick with tears.

'I think she mistook me for her dad. Proper scared the life out of me, she did. For a minute I thought my sins had finally caught up with me!' said the man as the woman slapped his arm and scowled at him.

'Oh, Lolly,' Mum sighed, stroking the back of my head.

'I so wanted it to be Dad, Mum,' I snuffled. 'I just want him to come home.'

'It's all my fault that Dad doesn't want to come back,' I told Zola on the bus to school on Monday morning.

'No it's not, Lolly, and you mustn't blame yourself,' she replied. 'How can it be your fault? You weren't even born when Mum was cheating on Dad.'

'But it's because she cheated and I'm not his daughter that he left.'

'Lolly, he'll come back,' said Zola, looking irritated. 'So please stop saying that he won't. You scare me when you say that.'

'Sorry,' I apologised.

'Whatever happened to thinking positively? That's what the old Lolly Luck, would say. She wouldn't be all down in the dumps like you're being now.'

'But that's just it – I'm not Lolly *Luck*, am I? Not really,' I replied gloomily. 'I feel like I don't belong in our family any more.'

'Of course you belong, Lolly, and you'll always be a Luck,' said Zola. 'Dad's probably still angry, which is pretty understandable because it came as a massive shock for him. He just needs more time to cool off, but he will be in touch. There's no way he'd abandon us.'

'How can you be so sure?'

'Because . . .' She paused. 'He just wouldn't, all right.'

Later on at school I had a rehearsal for the play, only things didn't go as well for me as they had done at the first rehearsal. Today my acting was dreadful. *Seriously* dreadful. Plus, I kept forgetting my lines. But since Dad had left, I'd hardly practised them.

'Are you all right, Lolly?' Mr Scott asked me after the rehearsal.

'Yes, sir, I'm fine,' I lied.

'And at home, are things OK?'

For a moment I felt like telling Mr Scott everything; how Dad had left because I wasn't his daughter and how I went from being the luckiest person I know to being completely unlucky, but instead I just said, 'Yes. Everything's fine at home.'

But he looked at me doubtfully. 'You didn't seem like you were enjoying the rehearsal at all. You forgot most of your lines, which makes me very worried,' he said. 'I know you're probably feeling the pressure of having the biggest part, but at the same time this play won't be a success if you can't remember your lines on the night.'

'I'm sorry, sir,' I mumbled, my cheeks feeling hot with embarrassment. 'It won't happen again.'

'Mr Kingsley did recommend that I give you an understudy,' said Mr Scott. 'When he first mentioned it I wasn't too keen, to tell you the truth, because I thought you'd be able to handle the part, no problem. But having seen how you performed today, I think I was right to agree to it.'

'But I don't need an understudy,' I burbled.

'Now, there's no need to be nervous about it, Lolly. Understudies are very common in the theatrical world. Many actors have them in case they fall ill or something goes wrong...'

'But nothing will go wrong, sir,' I said urgently.

'I understand and you are a good actress, Lolly. But I have to make sure that if any problems do occur, I have someone who can step into your role at a moment's notice. So that's why I've asked Mariella to be your understudy.'

'Mariella?!' I muttered, shocked.

'Yes, she's going to be your understudy. I offered her the role this morning and she accepted it right away.'

Hearing that Mariella was to be my understudy just felt like another sign that my luck had gone, and when the final bell went for school I couldn't wait to get home. I went back on my own as Zola went to Gita's for dinner and to do some revising for their end-of-year exams.

When Mum got in from work she cooked the two of us a chicken risotto for dinner, which made a change from all the ready-made pizzas she'd been feeding us since Gran had gone home.

'I wish he'd call,' she said as she ate slowly.

'Do you think he's OK, Mum? Safe, I mean?'

'I hope so, Lolly. Although I really thought he'd get in touch today considering its significance.'

I looked at Mum quizzically. 'How do you mean?'

She sighed. 'Well, on this day twenty years ago, your dad and I got married.'

'It's your anniversary!' I said as Mum's face drooped with sadness.

'It sure is, Lollipop, and it was the happiest day of my life.'

Then I heard myself saying, 'Mum, did you ever love Quincy?' And I wondered why since I didn't even want to talk about him. I didn't want to hear his name mentioned, either.

'It's your dad that I love, Lolly. He's my soulmate. I never loved Quincy and I should never have got involved with him.'

'But I wouldn't be here, though, would I? Do you wish I had never been born?'

'Of course not, Lolly, and please don't ever think that. I love you and Zola more than anything in the world,' she said, squeezing my hand.

'Do I look like him? Quincy?' I said, again wondering why I even cared.

'A bit,' said Mum quietly. 'You have his eyes.'

'Do I?' I made a face.

'You have very beautiful eyes, Lollipop. Quincy's a handsome man. And just then you reminded me of him. He used to screw up his face like that whenever a client annoyed him.'

'So, was he not a very nice person?' I asked.

'No, he was nice as it goes, funny too. I think he fancied himself as a bit of a comedian.'

'I want to meet him.'

Mum wrinkled her brow. 'Are you sure, Lollipop?' She looked at me intently. 'Actually, I don't think you're ready yet. Maybe in a couple of years the two of you—'

'I want to meet him,' I repeated taking a deep breath. 'I'm serious, Mum, I want to meet him.'

Chapter 9

Mum phoned Quincy, her voice ever so serious as they spoke about me meeting him. My heart was pounding, and for a second I felt like telling Mum to call it all off. I was petrified, but at the same time I really wanted to know more about him. It was like my whole life had suddenly become a jigsaw puzzle and he was the missing piece that would help me put it back together.

'Well, he's willing to meet you and he says he can be here on Saturday,' Mum told me when she'd come off the phone. 'And you're sure you're ready for this, Lolly? Because I can always call him back and tell him not to come if you prefer?'

I nodded my head firmly. 'I'm ready.'

'It feels like it's happening too quickly,' she said, brushing a hand over her hair. 'You're still trying to deal with your father leaving and now I'm introducing your real dad into your life. I'm scared it'll all be too much for you, Lollipop.'

'But I have to meet him, Mum. I need to know who I am.'

'You're Lolly Luck, that's who you are.'

'Yeah, but that's not what I—'

'It's OK, I know what you mean. Meeting him will help you gain a better sense of identity. I understand, but it doesn't stop me being worried.' She gave me a cuddle. 'But hopefully you'll like him. Quincy's a good man and he is looking forward to getting to know you and . . . um, Lolly, I think we better sit down.'

'Sit down. Why?'

'I have something else to tell you,' said Mum as we sat down on the sofa.

'Quincy said I should let you know before you meet up that you, erm . . . have two half-brothers.'

'I have brothers,' I said, looking at Mum in astonishment.

She smiled delicately. 'Yes. They're called Casper and Philip. I think Philip's the older one, but they're both younger than you. I expect Quincy will tell you more about them when you meet.'

I nodded slowly as I took it all in.

'So how does it feel knowing you're a big sister?' said Mum, staring at me expectantly.

'Oh, I'm not bothered,' I shrugged. But later on as I was getting ready for bed I couldn't help feeling a little excited at the thought of it. I'd always wanted to have younger siblings, and when I was smaller I used to imagine myself having pretend tea parties with my little brother or sister and teaching them how to make paper fans. Then I imagined them coming to me, their wise big sister, for advice on problems they needed solving as we grew up. As I fell asleep I wondered if Philip or Casper would ever come to me for advice, but, of course, we'd have to like each other first.

'Wow, two brothers!' said Nancy, when I told her about Casper and Philip the next day.

It was break time and we were standing at our favourite spot, beside the sinks in the girls' toilets.

'You're so lucky, Lolly. I wish I had a sister and two brothers, it sucks being an only child. So will you see them on Saturday too?'

'I'm not sure,' I said. 'But I tell you what, Nancy, it feels dead weird having a family I knew nothing about. Remember, it's not just Quincy and my brothers I haven't met yet, but cousins too, and uncles and aunties.'

'And how do you feel about Quincy? Do you still hate him?'

I shook my head as Mariella walked in. She smiled sweetly at Nancy, but gave me a sarcastic look which I swiftly returned. She went into one of the cubicles.

'I don't hate him but I am still angry,' I whispered so Mariella couldn't hear. 'He was the one who got my mum to cheat on my dad, don't forget, which was a very cruel thing to do. I should be *Dad's* daughter not his. So even if he does turn out to be a nice person, I'll never love him as much as I love Dad.'

Mariella came out of the cubicle and started washing her hands in one of the sinks.

'I like your earrings, Nancy,' she said, glancing at my friend's pink studs. 'They're very pretty.'

'Thanks,' said Nancy guardedly.

'You have rabbits, right?'

Nancy nodded.

'My mum and dad are buying me a rabbit as

a present for getting a part in the play,' said Mariella. 'Do you find them easy to look after?'

'Very easy,' said Nancy, her voice becoming excited. Rabbits were her favourite topic. 'I love my rabbits *so* much. They make the best pets. The only thing I don't enjoy is cleaning out their hutch, but me and my mum do that together now.'

'And do they bite?'

'Some rabbits might, but mine have never bitten anyone. They're very well-behaved.'

I raised my eyebrows at Nancy, but she failed to notice that I minded her talking to Mariella, who was definitely up to something.

'I've already picked out the rabbit I'm going to get,' Mariella continued. 'He's so sweet and he has these really cute spotty ears. But apparently he likes to climb on just about anything so my dad's going to rabbit-proof the house so he doesn't end up hurting himself.'

'Excuse me, but we *were* in the middle of a conversation before you rudely interrupted,' I told Mariella, my hands on my hips.

'Oh, I'm sorry,' she replied, not sounding the least bit sorry. 'I just wanted to ask Nancy a couple of questions, that's all.'

She flicked her hair over her shoulder, a vicious

smile creeping across her face. 'I forgot to say that I'm really excited about being your understudy, Lolly. Although I'm sure by the time the play arrives it'll be me who'll actually be playing Pollyanna.'

'No you won't!' said Nancy, springing to my defence. 'There's no way Mr Scott would give you the part. Lolly's a much better actress.'

But Mariella just laughed. 'You're kidding, right? Lolly, a good actress? *Purlease!*' she said and rolled her eyes at me. 'You're unreliable, Lolly. You forget your lines and you're just going to ruin this whole play. I should be Pollyanna, and I have a good feeling that I will be, very soon.'

She walked off towards the door, but then stopped and spun back round to face me. 'As they say in the acting profession, Lolly, break a leg. And I mean that. *Break a leg*,' she said and sauntered out.

'What a cow. But you mustn't let her get to you,' said Nancy.

Normally I could handle Mariella, but today wasn't one of those days. She *had* got to me. 'I can't stand her, I can't stand her, I can't stand her!'

'Me neither,' said Nancy. 'And I don't know why she was acting like I was her best friend all of a sudden, wanting to know about my rabbits.'

'So you noticed that too,' I was pleased.

'Mariella's such a fake. She'd love to break up our friendship. I bet she thinks that if she takes you away from me I'll be so upset I won't be able to act in the play.'

Nancy shook her head in disgust. 'She's the most jealous, meanest person at this school.'

'But what if Mr Scott *does* decide to give my part to her,' I said, gazing at my friend anxiously. 'She was right about me forgetting my lines. I forgot nearly all of them at the last rehearsal and Mr Scott wasn't pleased.'

'I'll help you out, Lolly. If you want, we'll go through your lines every lunch time, and Mariella, well, she won't have anything to say because you'll know them all off by heart.'

I smiled. 'Thanks, Nancy, you're a true friend.'

I didn't have my usual lie in on Saturday as Quincy was arriving at eleven o'clock and I had to be up before then. I was full of nerves, my stomach feeling like a giant pancake being flipped about.

'So today's the day, huh, when you finally get to meet Quincy,' said Zola as we ate breakfast together. 'How are you feeling?'

'I am a bit nervous. He's my biological dad, Zola, and I know nothing about him when I should know, well, everything. I don't even know if he's going to like me or if I'll like him.'

'He'll like you, don't worry. I would be here to give you some support only I'm going out in a bit. Me and Gita are going shopping, although I'll probably just be watching Gita doing the shopping since I've only got four quid. Anyway, I'm sure you'll have a nice day and you can tell me all about it when I get back.'

After breakfast I had a shower then changed into a pair of faded bootcut jeans and a very old yellow T-shirt. I didn't want Quincy to think I was making an effort for him. Mum wrinkled her nose when she saw me, but didn't suggest I put on something else as we waited for him to turn up. He arrived ten minutes early, the intercom bell literally startling us out of our seats.

Mum buzzed Quincy in and went to get the door.

'Hello, Marion,' I heard a voice bellow as she opened it.

My stomach churned faster as Mum walked back into the living room with the man who was my real dad.

The first thing I noticed about him was his height. He was very short, a bit shorter than Mum and much, much shorter than Dad. He was also very fat; his belly as big as Auntie Louise's when she was heavily pregnant with Mariah.

'Lolly, love, this is Quincy,' said Mum.

Quincy's lips curled up into a huge toothy grin and he stuck out his hand. 'Hello, Lollyanna. Pleased to meet you.'

I stared at him momentarily before giving his hand a limp shake.

Actually, he wasn't even much taller than me. In fact, if I stood on my toes we'd be the same height. Fingers crossed I took after my mum in the height department.

'So you live here, Marion?' said Quincy, his eyes surveying the room. 'Nice flat,' he added, but with a frown on his face.

'Thanks,' said Mum. 'No doubt your house is a lot more glamorous. Still driving the Rolls-Royce?'

'Nah, I upgraded a while back. Got myself a Lamborghini, didn't I?'

'A Lam-bor-ghi-ni,' said Mum, elongating the word and raising her eyebrows. 'Hmm, someone has gone up in the world.'

'Ever been in a Lamborghini, Lollyanna?' said Quincy.

I shook my head.

'Well you'll be going in one today and I think you'll love it. It's got a brilliant engine,' he said as he imitated the sound of a car.

'And still the comedian, I see,' said Mum.

'Well you know me, Marion, always up for the craic,' laughed Quincy, his fat stomach juddering up and down under his white shirt.

Mum laughed too, her eyes all soft and glowing. I didn't like the way she was looking at Quincy. It was a look she used to give Dad, a look that she shouldn't be giving another man.

'Although, if I recall correctly, you used to enjoy my car impersonations,' said Quincy.

Mum waggled her head. 'That was a long time ago, Quincy. A lot has changed since then. I'm not the same woman any more. But anyway, you're looking well. How's the PR business going?'

'Really good, thanks,' he said. 'I've got lots of clients and a great team working for me. And I love being my own boss. When you grow up, Lollyanna, make sure you find a job where you're working for yourself. That way it'll be you who gets to make the rules and you won't have to answer to tyrant chief executives like Mr Wickman – he was a man me and your mum used to work for. Remember him, Marion?'

'I certainly do.'

'So I was thinking that we could grab a bite to eat,' Quincy said to me. 'There's this fantastic Indian restaurant I used to go to back in the day which I think is still there. It's called something like the Regal, the Rogue . . .'

'I think you mean the Royal Tandoori,' said Mum, smiling. 'Yes it's still there, but I'm not sure you're going to be able to get a table. The restaurant's a lot more popular these days. You normally have to book at least a month in advance.'

'Really?' said Quincy, rubbing his chin. 'Still, there's no harm in us checking it out and if it's packed then Lolly and I can always go somewhere else.' He looked at me again. 'So, do you fancy checking out the Royal Tandoori?'

I shrugged. 'Yeah, OK.'

We all walked out into the hall. Mum picked up my jacket from the coat hook and crouched to help me into it, not that I needed help.

'I'll see you later, Lollipop,' she said, hugging me tightly. 'Enjoy your afternoon.'

Quincy and I took the lift down, but neither of us spoke. I wasn't sure what to say and it looked like Quincy had no idea, either, his eyes were firmly focused on the dirty lift floor.

When we got outside some boys from the estate were hanging around a black car that looked a lot like a racing driver's.

'This car is sick,' I could hear Joel, a boy I'd played out with a few times, say as we walked towards them.

Quincy pressed a black button attached to a key ring and the car doors opened upwards making the boys gasp in amazement. One of them got so excited that he started break dancing. I never realised a car could car create so much joy. But I couldn't have cared less about the silly thing. It didn't impress me.

'Good moves, son,' said Quincy.

'I'm so going to get a car like this when I grow up,' said Joel to his friends.

'Well, you'll need a very good job before you can afford a car like this,' said Quincy, 'so make sure you stay in school and get a decent education.'

It took Quincy two goes to actually get himself into the car, beads of sweat trickling down his forehead at the sheer hard work of it. I managed to get into the Lamborghini with ease, although it did take me a couple of seconds to get comfy in the slippery leather seat. The boys looked dead jealous.

‘Ready to go?’ said Quincy, his body all squashed up like a dumpling.

I shrugged.

‘I’ll take that as a yes, then.’

He put the key in the ignition and the car made the most horrendous sound.

‘Can you hear the roar?’ he asked, grinning.

I didn’t reply.

‘Stunning, isn’t it? Absolutely stunning,’ he said as we sped off noisily towards the restaurant.

When we got there I couldn’t believe how plush the place was. Silk curtains billowed next to massive windows, and above our heads, huge crystal chandeliers hung down from the ceiling. But even though it was great to finally be in the Royal Tandoori, it didn’t feel right being there without the rest of my family, especially as it was where we were supposed to have come to celebrate my birthday.

The restaurant was very busy, but Quincy and I were able to get a table as they’d had a late cancellation.

‘I’m a lucky man,’ chuckled Quincy to the smartly dressed waiter who showed us to our table, ‘so I can’t say I’m surprised that there was space for us.’

Maybe I really did get my luck from Quincy, when I still had it.

'So what would you like to have?' asked Quincy as we looked through the menu.

'I think I'll have the chilli sea bass,' I replied, remembering how good Dad had said it tasted.

'Well, I think I'm going to go for the chicken tikka masala,' chirped Quincy.

After a few minutes another waiter came over to take our order, which also included pilau rice, this lentil thing called tarka dal, two lemonades and poppadoms for starters.

'Right, Lollyanna, why don't you tell me a bit about yourself?' said Quincy when the waiter had left. 'Do you like your school?'

'Can you stop calling me Lollyanna? My name's *Lolly*,' I snapped as all my mixed-up feelings towards him began to bubble up inside of me. 'And, yes, I like my school.'

'Well that's good to hear, Lolly. And . . . um . . . do you have lots of friends?'

'Yes.'

'Excellent. And what's your favourite subject?'

'I don't have one.'

'My favourite subject was chemistry,' Quincy continued as the waiter brought over our lemonades. 'I used to love doing experiments, mixing different chemicals together to make fizzy gases.' He paused.

'When I spoke to your mum again she said you got a part in your school play. You're playing Pollyanna, right?'

I nodded dully as I drank some of my lemonade.

'I imagine you've been doing lots of rehearsing. How's that all been going?'

'Fine,' I said abruptly.

The waiter returned with our poppadoms and some pickles to go with them. Quincy picked one up and munched on it quickly. It was obvious he was trying to think of something more to say.

'Would you like to hear a joke, Lolly?' was all he could come up with.

I narrowed my eyes. 'What joke?'

'Why, the one about the astronaut. Do you know what part of the computer he likes best?'

I shrugged and glanced round the restaurant. I tried to see if I could spot a few celebrities, but sadly there weren't any.

'It's the space bar!' Quincy exclaimed.

I didn't laugh, which made Quincy shuffle about in his chair, his face tensing up.

'I expect your mum mentioned that I also have two sons. Philip's seven and Casper recently turned five. We all live in Southend with my wife, Jumoke, their mum. I met her when I moved there a little while after you were born. They're all looking forward to meeting you, Lolly.'

'Southend? That's where I thought my great-uncle Ernest lived until I found out he was you. Why did you pretend to be someone else?' I said.

'It's all very complicated, Lollyanna – sorry, Lolly. When I found out your mum was pregnant, I agreed not to have any contact with you, but I was adamant that I'd support you financially. I know the money I used to send you for your birthday and Christmas wasn't much, but now that everything's out in the open I'd like to start giving you more, if that's OK with you. Or you can just tell me the type of stuff that you like and I'll buy it for you. Philip's into anything to do with Transformers. He's got all the toys, you know. Is there a particular doll you like?'

'Dolls are for babies,' I scoffed.

'Oh, right,' muttered Quincy, tapping his fingers together. 'Well, if there is something that you'd like, do let me know – and don't worry about the cost. I've got plenty of money.'

He cleared his throat. 'I really would like us to get to know each other, Lolly. I know I haven't been a part of your life up until now but I am ready to be a proper dad to you if you'll let me.

And I mean it, if there's anything you want just let me know and I'll get it for you.'

'I want my parents to get back together. Can you magic that up for me?' I shouted, which made people stare at us.

Quincy looked taken aback, and for a few moments he didn't say a thing.

'Your mum did tell me she and Austin were having some time apart, and I'm sure it's been a very difficult time for you,' he said after a short while. 'But, Lolly, I do think him finding out the truth was the right thing. He probably wants to punch my lights out…' He hesitated. 'I guess it's just going to take your mum and Austin a bit of time before they patch things up.'

When we'd finished our poppadoms, the waiter came over and took away the empty poppadom basket before bringing over my chilli sea bass and Quincy's curry. The sea bass smelled lovely, and Dad was right, it was tremendous.

'Why did you give me three hundred pounds for my eleventh birthday?' I asked Quincy. 'You didn't normally give me that amount when you were pretending to be Great-Uncle Ernest.'

Quincy nodded his head. 'You're right, but I guess I just reached a point where I thought, no way am I going to give you a measly fifty pounds twice a year. I know it was what your mum and I agreed I'd pay, but to me you deserve much more than that. You see, I want you to be able to have the best things in life, Lolly. And like I said, I've got plenty of money.'

'Did you love my mum?' I asked Quincy, which had him coughing out bits of chicken.

'I was fond of her,' he said, his voice hoarse. 'She meant a lot to me so, yes, I guess you could say there was a time when I loved her.'

'Do you love me?'

'I . . . er . . . don't really know you, Lolly,' he stammered. 'Oh, what am I saying? Of course I love you; you're my daughter.'

He ducked a hand into one of his trouser pockets, pulling out a wallet.

'I like to carry this everywhere I go,' he said, taking a photo of me out of the wallet. I was standing in front of the Christmas tree we had last year, smiling brightly in my favourite yellow jumper. 'I put a new photo in here every year. You're growing up into such a beautiful young lady, Lolly. And I've also kept the fans you'd send, which for a long time felt like the only connection I had with you, until now.'

'You shouldn't have pretended to be my uncle,' I quickly snapped at him. 'You made my sister really sad not sending her cards and money. She thought Great-Uncle Ernest didn't like her.'

'She wasn't my child to give money to,' he whispered. 'But you are, and I'm so proud of you, Lolly.'

'I'm not going to call you "Dad", if that's what you're thinking.'

'I wouldn't expect you to. Austin's your dad; he's the one who's been looking after you all these years. But I'd still like to be there for you, Lolly. I also wanted to ask you something. Would you like to meet your brothers?'

'Can I?' I said, a little too excitedly. But I did really want to meet them.

Quincy grinned. 'Sure you can. They can't wait to meet you. How does next weekend sound? You can join us in Southend and we can all go down to the beach. Or is that too soon?'

'No, next weekend's fine,' I said, keeping my voice casual this time.

'Great. Of course, I'll have to speak to your mum and check that it's OK with her.'

He started to giggle. 'I've just thought of another joke,' he said, rubbing his hands together. 'Where do rocks like to spend their holidays?'

'I don't know. Where *do* rocks like to spend their holidays?'

'Pebble beach!' he said and made a funny face.

I rolled my eyes. 'That is so lame.'

'I know, I know. But you can't blame a man for trying,' he laughed.

'But even I know better jokes than that,' I said as I quickly tried to think of one. 'Why can't a leopard hide?'

'You tell me, why can't a leopard hide?'

'Because he's always spotted!'

'Mmm, not bad, but I'd say my joke was better,' said Quincy.

He laughed again and suddenly I was laughing too, so much so that it felt like my tummy was going to burst.

'Would you like to come to my school play?' I found myself saying as I tried to catch my breath.

But immediately I wished I hadn't said it, because I wasn't sure that I did want Quincy at my play. It was Dad I wanted in the audience, watching attentively and clapping with pride at the end as I took a bow. But it was too late.

'I'd love to come,' said Quincy grinning.

*

When I got home Mum wanted to know how it all went.

'OK,' I told her, dithering slightly.

She smiled. 'And what do you think of him?'

I shrugged. I did like Quincy, sort of, but I couldn't help feeling that by liking him I was being disloyal to Dad. 'He's OK.'

Mum's smile wobbled. I think she was hoping for a more detailed response.

'Well, I'm glad it went well,' she said, nodding uncertainly.

I told Zola about my afternoon while she was showing me the new top she'd bought with her four pounds. I told her Quincy was short and fat, which made her laugh and say, 'What did Mum see in him?' Then I told her about how rich he was and that he drove a Lamborghini and she kissed her teeth like Gran and said, 'She was probably after his money.'

'That's an evil thing to say, Zola,' I told her. But she just glared at me and said, 'So, what other reason did Mum have to cheat on Dad?'

For moment I thought about this question myself, but all I could do was frown and say that I didn't know. I also told Zola that I'd invited Quincy to the play, but she reckoned that was a crazy thing for me to have done.

'He's not family!' she said furiously. 'I can't believe you invited him. How could you do that, Lolly? Only family should be there.'

'I know,' I said, feeling a little confused. Surely being my real dad meant that Quincy *was* now my family?

'I do want Dad to be there, Zola,' I insisted, even though I had no idea of how I was going to get him to come, or if I was even ever going to see him again.

Chapter 10

The next day I couldn't believe it when we finally got the call we'd be waiting weeks for, or should I say *Zola* got the call. Still, I couldn't have been more pleased when Dad phoned home. Zola spent ages talking to him, and it was so frustrating because she wouldn't let me on so I could have my own little chat.

'When is he coming home?' I was practically begging her to tell me, but she just made a rude face and put a finger to her lips.

The next thing I knew she was ordering me to go into the kitchen to get her a glass of orange juice and then to our bedroom to fetch a pen and paper. I wasn't too happy about being her little servant, but I did it anyway and glumly watched as Zola gulped back the juice and scribbled down whatever Dad was telling her to write. Then suddenly she said, 'I love you too,' which meant Dad was about to come off the phone.

I sprinted over. 'My turn,' but it was too late, Dad had hung up.

'You knew I wanted to speak to him!' I fumed.

'He had to go out,' was the excuse she gave.

I sighed. 'You mean he didn't want to talk to me.'

'Don't be silly, Lolly,' said Zola putting her head to one side. 'He really did have to go out. He said something about having to meet someone about a job. It was probably one of those consultants.'

'Well, did he mention me, you know, that he missed me?' I asked, a hopeful expression on my face.

'Yeah, course. He misses you, he misses all of us,' said Zola breezily. But I wasn't convinced.

'When I see him, I'm going to tell him that I love him loads and loads, and that he's the best dad in the whole wide world and that I only want him to be my dad and not Quincy,' I said in a rush.

'Well, that's good, only, don't mention that you invited Quincy to your play,' said Zola, shaking her head at me. 'I still can't believe you did that, you know. I mean, what will Dad say when he finds out? He'll be dead upset, Lolly.'

'I know I shouldn't have invited him, Zola,' I retorted, 'so please stop going on about it. I already told you that I never meant to invite Quincy. I just sort of said it. And I wouldn't have invited him if Dad had got in touch with us sooner.'

'Well, I'm sure Dad will want to come, which means you're going to have to uninvite Quincy,' said Zola, her voice curt.

'OK!' I huffed even though I wasn't sure how I was actually going to do it. I'd never uninvited someone from something before, not like Mariella Sneddon who was always uninviting kids from her birthday parties if she'd fallen out with them. She did that to me when we fell out over her butterfly clip, which meant I was the only person in our class who didn't get the chance to go to her bowling-night birthday party.

'Anyway, where *is* Dad?' I asked, changing the subject.

'He's staying at a B&B,' said Zola and held up the piece of paper she'd written on. 'He gave me the address.'

I smiled. 'It will be good to see him, Mum's

going to be so happy when we tell her. Do you reckon we should phone her on her mobile or wait until she gets back from the shops?'

'No, Lolly, we can't tell her,' said Zola, her eyes levelling with mine. 'Dad doesn't want to see Mum.'

'But you just said he was missing us – all of us.'

'I know, but I don't think he can deal with seeing her right now. And he told me that he doesn't want us to tell her where he is, either. You're going to have to keep it a secret.'

'Keep it a secret?' I said, surprised. 'But she misses him, Zola, we have to tell her.'

'Do you want to see Dad or not?' said Zola sharply. 'Because if we tell her, he might disappear again. So I really need you to keep your mouth shut, Lolly.'

She folded the piece of paper and put it in the back pocket of her jeans.

'I want to see Dad tomorrow, so we'll go straight after school. He says the B&B is near our old high street so it shouldn't take us too long to get there.'

'I'm going to give my dad a huge, huge hug,' I told Nancy as we spoke about him the following day at lunch.

'Are you going to tell him you met up with Quincy?' she asked, tucking into her cheese salad.

I shook my head. 'No, I don't think I should. It might upset him because he might think I prefer Quincy to him.' I paused. 'I'm also going to have to think of a fib that I can tell Quincy so he doesn't come to the play cos my dad won't come if he knows Quincy's going to be there too.'

'Why don't you just tell Quincy that the school didn't give out enough tickets?' suggested Nancy. 'That doesn't sound much like a fib.'

'I guess I could,' I mulled it over as Mariella and Trinity approached the table plonking themselves down.

I narrowed my eyes. 'If you've come over to show off about being my understudy, well, I don't want to hear it. I'm not interested.'

'Don't worry, I wasn't going to,' said Mariella, a false smile on her face. 'I wanted to speak to Nancy again,' she looked at my friend. 'Me and my dad bought the hutch for my rabbit at the weekend. I can't wait until I finally get to bring him home.'

'Good for you,' said Nancy coldly.

'I know, aren't I lucky?' trilled Mariella not at all miffed by Nancy's hostile response. She focused her attention back on me. 'By the way, I know all of Pollyanna's lines now.'

'I don't care, Mariella,' I said, but really I did.

'I helped Mariella learn her lines. I think she's going to be a wonderful Pollyanna,' said Trinity.

'Well, I've been learning my lines too, with Nancy's help,' I retorted. I looked over to the teachers' table. 'I'm going to show Mr Scott that I can be the best Pollyanna this school has ever seen.'

Mariella and Trinity looked at each other sceptically.

'Well, Mr Scott says he wants to have a rehearsal with me playing Pollyanna,' said Mariella.

Over her shoulder I could see Mr Scott getting up from the teachers' table, his lunch box in his hand. He waved goodbye to the other teachers and began walking in our direction.

'He never said anything to me about that,' I responded.

'Nor me,' said Nancy.

'Oh, it's true,' said Mariella. 'And when the rehearsal happens, that der-brain will realise he made a huge mistake in casting you in the role and he'll give the part to me. My parents are going to be so proud to see me in the starring role.'

'That's not nice calling Mr Scott a der-brain,' said Nancy, fully aware that our teacher was now only a metre away.

'Sooooo?' purred Mariella. 'I can call him what I like. He *is* a der-brain, everyone knows that.'

Mr Scott was now standing right behind Trinity and Mariella.

'If he wasn't, then he would've noticed that I copied all of Trinity's answers in that English test we did the other day.'

'You cheated in the test!' I gasped as Mr Scott raised his eyebrows, continuing to silently listen in.

Mariella shrugged casually. 'Yeah. So what? I've done it loads of times since Mr Spock's been our teacher. And the fact that he still hasn't sussed it out makes him the biggest der-brain in this entire school.'

Mr Scott looked livid, his face turning fire-engine red. He nodded at me to carry on, and I did.

'Why did you just call Mr Scott, "Mr Spock"?' I asked carefully.

'Duh, because he looks like Spock,' said Mariella rolling her eyes. 'Omigod, have you never seen *Star Trek*?'

'Mr Scott's ears are so weird and pointy, just like Spock's,' Trinity added, pulling a face.

'Yeah, talk about being a freakoid,' said Mariella giggling.

Mr Scott looked like he was about to explode. He cleared his throat. Mariella and Trinity's faces froze.

'*Freakoid*, eh?' he said as they slowly turned their heads round to face him. 'I don't think I've heard that word before. And what else did you say I was?'

Mariella bit her lip, her eyes blinking up at him.

'A *der-brain*, that's it,' Mr Scott answered for her. 'I'm a der-brain and I also look like Spock from *Star Trek*. Well, I never. I used to think I looked more like Captain Kirk myself, but I guess I got it wrong.'

He laughed but his face was deadly serious.

'W-w-we were only joking, sir,' stammered Mariella.

'Were you now?' said Mr Scott, his eyebrows furrowed. 'Only, you didn't sound like you were joking. You sounded very serious to me, especially the bit where you admitted you'd cheated in the English test.'

'I-I-I didn't cheat. I didn't, sir, I didn't,' said Mariella, shaking her head profusely.

I was trying my best not to laugh, but it was proving really difficult since I'd been waiting for this moment for a long time. Finally, Mariella Sneddon was going to get her comeuppance. Still, I did all I could to keep my laughter in, squeezing my lips together so it couldn't escape.

'Do you know what, Mariella?' said Mr Scott, a hand under his chin. 'I think I might have got a bit ahead of myself when I made you the understudy for Pollyanna. You see, I'm not sure you're the right type of person to understudy. In fact, I'm not sure you're the right type of person that should be playing Mrs Tarbell, either. I don't think I want cheats in my play.'

'But it only happened the once, sir, I swear,' blustered Mariella. 'Please don't stop me from being in the play. My parents are going to be so cross with me.'

'She *made* me give her the answers,' Trinity suddenly blurted out. 'She said she wouldn't be my friend if I didn't let her copy them.'

'I think the three of us need to pay Mr Kingsley a visit, don't you?' said Mr Scott as he ushered the two of them up. They nodded sullenly and followed him out of the hall to the head's office.

As soon as they were out of earshot Nancy and I finally burst out laughing.

'Serves her right, the big cheat,' I said.

'And now you don't have to worry about her playing Pollyanna,' said Nancy as we shared a smile.

Zola was waiting for me at the gates when school finished and we took a bus into town. It was only a ten-minute journey, but when we got off we hadn't a clue how to get to the B&B. We had no map, just the address: Kelmore Close. We ended up going from shop to shop asking for directions. It was knackering, and most of the shopkeepers seemed to have no idea where Kelmore Close was, either. But luckily one did – the owner of a key-cutting shop. He was very helpful and gave us really detailed directions. He told us we needed to turn into a road where there was a church before turning into another road that had a house on the corner 'which you can't miss' because it was painted bright orange. Then we had to take the second road on the right and then the first road on the left, walk to the very end of that road where we'd find the B&B on the right-hand side of the street. His directions made my head spin. It was much too complicated for me, but Zola was happy to lead the way.

She did a really good job of finding all those roads, and when we finally got to Kelmore Close, we ran towards the B&B as though our lives depended on it. The Three Kings Hotel it was called, though I doubt any kings would want to stay there. It was dead shabby, the front garden full of weeds, the windows sheathed with dirt. But I guess it was all my dad could afford. As we walked inside half of me couldn't wait to see him while the other half was scared to bits. Would Dad even want to see me? I wasn't sure I'd be able to handle it if he rejected me. We went up to the reception desk. A woman wearing a ruffly green blouse was talking into the telephone.

'Just a minute,' she said to us, holding up her hand and continuing her conversation. 'I know! I couldn't believe it when she told me. I mean, what a flaming cheek expecting her to pay for their holiday. I told her to dump him, but you know Sam, never listens. It's just like the time I told her that Versace dress didn't go with her eye shadow. But she still insisted on wearing the dress and all it did was make her look like an Oompa-loompa.'

'Excuse me,' said Zola.

'I'll be with you in a minute,' said the woman, swivelling her chair away from us.

I wondered how many more minutes she planned on making us wait.

'No, I'm not going clubbing this weekend,' she nattered down the phone. 'Neil has a surprise treat planned for me. I've been begging him to tell me what it is, but I suppose it would spoil it if he did. I've got a feeling it's a trip to London, probably to see that musical Bev's been talking about.'

'Is Mr Luck here?' Zola asked loudly, an annoyed look spreading across her face.

The woman swivelled back towards us.

'We don't do raised voices in here, young miss,' she said, glaring at us fixedly. 'This hotel might not have any stars after its name, but we do still consider ourselves to be a respectable establishment.'

'Is Mr Luck here, pleassssse,' cooed Zola caustically.

'Jen, I've got to go, hun, but I'll call you back, I promise. Bye, honey, bye,' said the woman and put down the phone.

She dazzled us with a fake smile, chewing gum poking out between her teeth. 'So, you want to see Mr Luck, do you?'

'Yes,' said Zola, screwing up her lips.

'And you are?'

'His daughters,' Zola told her.

The woman straightened herself in the chair. 'I'm not sure he's in but I'll give him a call,' she said stiffly.

She dialled the number for his room. 'Oh, hello, Mr Luck, it's Mandy on reception here. I have two girls with me who say they're your daughters... Send them up? OK, will do.'

She put down the phone. 'Go to the third floor and it's the second door on your left,' she clucked on her gum. 'There's a lift over there if you want to take it.'

She pointed to a set of silver doors. We walked across and I pressed the button to call the lift. But it was taking for ever to come down from the fourth floor so we went up the stairs instead.

Dad was standing at the doorway of his room when we reached his floor. He smiled at us wearily as he reached out and hugged Zola and then me.

I'm sure my hug wasn't as long as his hug with Zola. But I quickly told myself I was just being silly cos it's not as if I'd actually counted the seconds of both our hugs, but as we walked into Dad's room I couldn't stop myself from wondering if he now loved Zola more than he loved me.

'Welcome to my lovely new abode, girls,' said Dad as he shut the door behind us.

But I think he was being sarcastic because the room was definitely not lovely. In fact, it was a complete mess with clothes strewn all over the place, along with balled-up tissues and plastic takeaway boxes filled with gloopy leftover food. I think the last meal he must've eaten was sweet-and-sour chicken because the room had a very distinct sweet-and-sour whiff to it, though the sour smell may have been from the dirty socks that were hanging off his bedside table.

'So how have you been?' Zola asked as we sat down on his untidy bed.

I had to sit up again, because a plastic fork was poking me in the bum.

'Well, I am feeling a bit better than when I first got here,' said Dad, nodding his head tiredly. 'Do excuse the mess, girls. I'm afraid I haven't had a chance to do much tidying up this week. The hotel cleaner normally does it, but she's gone off sick, apparently.'

'We miss you, Dad, and we really want you back,' I said. 'When are you going to come home?'

'I don't know,' he replied, directing his answer at Zola. 'I've missed you too, but, as you know, things are very strained between me and your mother at the moment. Plus, I still need time to get my head around . . . everything.'

'Oh, please come home, Dad,' said Zola. 'I need you more than ever right now. I have my end-of-year exams soon and I've really been stressing out about them. I'm scared I'm going to mess up.'

'You won't, sweetheart. You'll do well and make me proud like you always do. And if you are worried then you can always pick up the phone and give me a call.'

'But we've been calling you for weeks, Dad! You haven't been answering. I was scared you might be dead,' said Zola and she started to cry.

'I'm sorry, darling, that I didn't ring and let you know I was OK,' said Dad, wrapping an arm around her. 'I wanted to, and there were so many times that I picked up the phone and was about to dial the number, but I'd always end up chickening out. I was full of so many emotions that I hadn't a clue of what I was even going to say to you. But I'll never disappear like that again, I promise. I'm not as upset as I was and I think things are looking up for me again. I even had a job interview.'

'That's great, Dad,' I said, but he didn't look at me.

Maybe it was all in my head but it did feel like Dad didn't want me there. I know he said he missed *us* but perhaps it was Zola he'd really missed. She was his real daughter, I guess, unlike me who probably meant nothing to him any more.

'So, how's school?' Dad asked Zola.

'It's been OK,' she told him. 'But guess what? Mr Drury's leaving.'

'Really?' said Dad intrigued. 'He's been at Greenwood High for years. You kids won't find a head teacher as good as him I can tell you. He's one of the best in the county.'

'But he can be so overbearing, Dad,' said Zola. 'You know how the school colours are yellow and blue? Well, the other day you should've seen the way he was going on at me because I had a *gold* scrunchie in my hair. But gold is the same colour as yellow, right? Then he said that if I didn't take it out, he'd exclude me for the day. I mean, has the man never heard of fashion?'

For several minutes Dad chatted to Zola about her head teacher and her exams, and all the while he said nothing to me.

I interrupted them. 'Mrs Avery had her baby, Dad. She sent the class a photo last week. You should see him, he's soooo cute. He's called Oliver.'

'Well done, Mrs Avery,' said Dad, getting up and going over to open the window.

'And you'll never guess what happened at school today, Dad. It was well funny. Me and Nancy were having lunch when Mariella Sneddon comes over and starts going on about how she reckons Mr Scott is going to let her play Pollyanna instead of me. Then she starts calling him a der-brain and saying how he looks like Spock from *Star Trek*, and how he hadn't even noticed that she'd cheated in our English test. But she didn't realise that Mr Scott was right behind her. You should've seen him, Dad, he was so cross and Mariella was like, "*Oh, Mr Scott, I didn't cheat, I didn't cheat.*" And now she's in big trouble.'

'It looks like it might rain,' said Dad. He hadn't been listening to a word I'd been saying. 'Did you girls bring an umbrella?'

'No,' said Zola.

'I'll give you mine before you go.' He turned back round and sat down again.

'So what's this hotel like?' I asked cautiously.

'The only good thing here is the breakfast,' he replied, glancing round the room. 'The bathroom resembles something out of a horror film and I daren't get in the lift. I hope you girls didn't come up in it?'

'We took the stairs,' said Zola.

'Good, because it shakes so much that you're convinced the cables will snap and the lift will go hurtling down to the ground. The couple who run this place have no interest in sorting it out and they're always getting complaints.'

He looked up at the ceiling and shook his head.

'I've got the play coming up soon,' I said. 'We've had lots of rehearsals, although one didn't go so well, but I'm really excited. Do you think you'll be able to come, Dad? I'd love you to be there.'

'I'll have to see,' he mumbled, looking at his hands. 'If I do get the job I mentioned, the company might want me to work, so I can't guarantee anything just yet, Lollipop. But I'll try my best to make it.'

'Cool, thanks, Dad,' I said, feeling a bit happier.

Zola tried to catch my eye. 'But *he'll* be there, remember,' she whispered.

'Who'll be there?' said Dad.

'No one,' I said.

'Is it Quincy? You've not invited him, have you?'

I hesitated.

Dad's face crumpled. 'Right, so he's on the scene...?' he said, finally looking at me, his eyes ever so sad. 'Wants to be a father to you, does he, after eleven years?' He snorted.

'No, Dad, he doesn't,' I replied quickly. 'And

he won't be coming to my play. I just want you there. You, Mum and Zola.'

Dad checked his watch.

'It's getting on, girls, and no doubt your mother will be wondering where you are,' he said. 'But you can come again if you like. I'll call you and we'll arrange a time.'

He stood up and Zola rushed into his arms.

'I really want you to come home, Dad,' she whimpered.

'I know, sweetheart, I know.'

I went up to Dad too, but he didn't reach out his arms to embrace me. So all I could do was just stand there, looking on, feeling daft and totally left out.

'Mum misses you,' I said and instantly regretted that I had. Dad's face turned furious.

'She mustn't know that I'm here, do you understand?' he growled. 'I said, *do you understand*?'

I nodded twice. 'I understand. I won't say a thing, I promise,' I muttered, blinking hard to fight back the tears that were about to pour out.

'I can't face her right now,' he said as he fetched us his umbrella then walked over to the door and held it open.

'Take care, girls, and I'll see you soon.'

I looked at Dad again but he wouldn't meet my eye. I waited until we were out of the B&B before I burst into tears.

Chapter 11

My dad hated me. I was sure of it, but I couldn't convince Zola that I wasn't exaggerating.

'He *was* different with me, Zola,' I tried to explain to her on the bus back home. 'He didn't want to speak to me; he didn't even want to look at me, Zola. And he was *so* cross.'

'Dad doesn't hate you, Lolly. You're being paranoid,' she responded. 'But if he was angry then I'm not surprised. You did invite the man who Mum cheated on him with to your school play, so, of course, Dad's going to be a little furious, don't you think? Plus, you hardly know Quincy. You've only met him once.'

'I know I made a mistake in inviting Quincy and I'm going to fix it. But you shouldn't have opened your big mouth, Zola. Dad wouldn't have known about it if you'd kept quiet.'

'Don't blame me, Lolly Loser! This isn't my fault, you know,' sniped my sister, which made me start crying again.

She quickly apologised. 'Look, if Dad really is cross then it won't last,' she whispered as she gently patted my back. 'He did say he wanted us to visit him again, and when we do you'll see that you got this all wrong, Lolly. Dad loves you.'

Despite what Zola said I still had my doubts, and over the next few days all I could think about was the look Dad had given me when I'd mentioned Mum. It was the angriest he'd ever been with me and it was as if I'd suddenly become this horrible little creature that he wanted to eject out of his life.

So when Saturday arrived I couldn't help feeling a little relieved. A day at the seaside seemed like just the thing I needed to cheer myself up.

Quincy turned up at ten o'clock on the dot, and once I'd given Zola and Mum a hug goodbye, we were off, driving down the motorway towards Southend. Quincy asked me how school was going and I told him all about this persuasive-writing project I was doing where I had to write a pretend advert to promote a made-up new cereal.

He told me about a party his company had organised for a new men's clothes shop. Apparently loads of celebrities were there, including Corey T. *He'd met Corey T!* And not only that but he knew Corey T's manager. I was gobsmacked. I told him how much I loved Corey T, and Quincy promised he'd call his manager to see if he could send me some VIP tickets to one of his upcoming concerts.

I was ecstatic and when we got out of the car at Southend, I threw my arms around him. 'Thank you, thank you, thank you!' I squealed.

He hugged me back. It felt so comforting and reminded me of the hugs that Dad used to give me.

'Daddy, Daddy!' a voice suddenly boomed.

We turned round as a boy with a mohican haircut ran towards us.

Quincy bent and scooped the boy up into his arms. 'Where's Mummy?' Quincy asked him.

'Oh, she's coming,' he replied, pointing at a woman and another boy further down the road.

'Casper, I'd like you to meet your sister, Lolly,' said Quincy.

'I don't want a sister.' Casper stuck out his bottom lip.

I swallowed. It wasn't quite the reaction I'd hoped for. Quincy laughed, although I couldn't see what was so funny. Still, I remained polite.

'It's nice to meet you, Casper,' I said. 'You have the same name as Casper the friendly ghost. I love that cartoon.'

'I am not a ghost,' the little boy replied fiercely.

I bit my lip as my other brother approached. He too had a mohican haircut, but was much thinner than Casper who was chubby like his dad. He smiled sheepishly as Quincy introduced us.

'And this is my wife, Jumoke,' Quincy told me as the woman shook my hand.

Jumoke was very glamorous. She looked like a model and she towered over Quincy in her stylish suit and sandals. But I don't think her long black hair was her own – it looked like a wig.

'Lolly! We meet at last. And, heavens, don't you look like your dad?' she said smiling. 'You have the same cute big ears,' she added, making me burn with embarrassment.

I *so* do not have big ears.

'*She* doesn't look like Daddy. I do,' squawked Casper, pulling on his own ears defiantly. 'See,

I have his ears!' His mum and dad laughed.

'So, Lolly, what do you fancy doing today?' asked Quincy.

I had a little think before telling him I wanted to go to the funfair and then down to the beach.

'Yay! Let's go to the funfair,' said Casper. 'I want to go on the bumper cars.'

So we all wandered up to the fairground, Casper walking between his mum and dad while I walked beside Philip. I tried to make conversation with my brother, but straightaway it was clear that Philip wasn't the talkative type. I asked him if he had any hobbies, but all I got back was 'Um, um, um'. I asked him if he enjoyed living in Southend only to get some more um um ums. So I decided not to ask him any more questions.

When we reached the bumper cars I climbed into my own, as did Quincy and Philip, while Casper shared a car with his mum. At first it was great zooming around with music pumping through the speakers, but then Casper started to bump my car, really hard. I'm sure he was doing it on purpose. He had this mean look in his eyes while his mother just sat there shrieking with laughter, her fake hair blowing across her face. I tried to escape them by driving in the opposite direction, only Casper kept coming after me.

I couldn't wait for it to be over, and when the cars slowed to a halt, I quickly jumped out, my neck aching from all the bumps.

'Again, again! I want to go again,' chanted Casper.

'OK, son, but let's see what your sister would like to do,' said Quincy. 'Lolly, do you fancy another go?'

'No thanks,' I replied and rubbed my neck.

'OK, well we can try something else.'

'Why do we have to do what she wants?' groaned Casper, his arms crossed.

'Because, darling, this is Lolly's treat today,' said Jumoke patting him on the head. 'She doesn't live near the seaside like you do. You have the chance to come here all the time.'

We walked over to some stalls, stopping at one that had lots of teddies as prizes. To win one you had to score fifteen or more points by getting hoops around these bowling pins with numbers on them.

'Do you fancy a go, little man?' the guy on the stall asked Casper.

He nodded excitedly as the man handed him four hoops.

But Casper wasn't very good at the game. Quincy paid for him to have lots of goes, but he wasn't able to get any of his hoops around the pins.

'Can I try?' I offered.

'Sure, why not,' said Quincy as he paid the stall holder some more money.

The stall-holder guy then gave me four hoops and when I threw the first one, I immediately got it around a pin that had the number five on it. I quickly threw my second hoop, but that missed all the pins completely. I concentrated a bit harder as I threw my third hoop, which landed around a pin that had the number six on it. I then threw my last hoop – it glided through the air before dropping down onto the same pin. I'd done it, I'd scored seventeen points!

'Well, I never,' said the stall holder, taking off his cap and fanning himself with it. 'You made that look easy-peasy. Now then, which teddy bear would you like?'

I pointed at a yellow bear with a brown button nose. The man took it down from the shelf and put it into my arms.

'Well done, Lolly,' said Philip and his mum.

'Thanks,' I said as Quincy put a hand on my shoulder.

'That's my girl,' he said, which felt strange, because even though he was my real dad, I didn't see myself as *his* girl. I was still *Dad's* girl, whether he loved me or not.

We walked across to another stall where, to win a prize, you had to get a plastic ball through the mouth of one of the painted lions. There were teddy hippos, teddy giraffes and teddy gorillas, as well as hula-hoops, footballs, skipping ropes, and a prize I had my eye on: a huge teddy penguin.

'Philip, why don't you have a go at this game?' Quincy called his son over.

'Philip's wonderful at throwing,' he whispered to me as the stall-holder lady gave his son a ball. 'He won't miss, mark my words.'

Philip missed – three times. He wanted to have a fourth go, but Casper snatched the ball from him.

'My turn,' he bleated, but unfortunately his ball missed too.

'Your turn, Lolly,' said Quincy, plopping more coins into the stall holder's hands.

'Casper, would you like to hold my bear while I have a go?' I asked my brother.

'Urgh, no way do I want to hold that rubbish bear!' he replied swiftly.

'Hey, don't be so cheeky, Casper,' said Quincy.

'Here, Lolly. I'll take your bear for you,' he added as I handed it over to him.

I picked up a ball and threw it quickly. It was a pathetic throw, but it went straight through a lion's mouth.

'Yay!' I screeched.

'Congratulations, young lady!' said the stall-holder lady. 'And as you got the ball through the lion with the smallest mouth that entitles you to one of my top prizes.'

'Can I have the penguin, please?' I said, and she went and fetched it for me.

I hadn't felt this lucky in ages. It was like my old luck had suddenly returned. Perhaps it hadn't really gone at all. Maybe it'd just been hiding itself.

'Here you go,' said the woman handing over the teddy penguin that was so big I almost toppled over.

'Here let me help,' Jumoke offered, taking the teddy penguin and carrying it for me. We moved on to the stall next door, which was selling an assortment of nick-nacks and jewellery.

Casper picked up a gold ring with a pink diamond in the middle.

'Yuck,' I heard him say under his breath. But I thought it looked quite nice.

I picked up a small blue box that had a pair of gold teardrop earrings in it.

'Pretty, aren't they?' said Quincy. 'Would you like me to get them for you?'

I nodded. 'Thanks, Quincy.'

He grinned. 'I think they'll suit you.'

He gave the stall holder a ten-pound note and the earrings were mine.

'Those are nice,' said Jumoke as I put them in.

'Yes, they're lovely,' I replied.

'No they're not. They're ugly just like you,' said Casper cruelly.

'Stop that!' shouted Quincy. 'That's a horrible thing to say. And I don't understand why you're behaving like this, Casper. This morning you couldn't wait to see Lolly, but since we got here you've been nothing but rude to her. Now say you're sorry.'

'Sorry, Lolly,' said Casper, but as soon as Quincy's back was turned he poked his tongue out at me.

'Lunch time!' said Quincy, rubbing his hands together.

'Can I have a burger, Daddy?' said Philip, pointing at a van opposite us.

'Would you like a burger, Lolly?' asked Quincy.

I nodded and we all wandered over.

'Hello there,' said the man in the burger van. 'And what will it be? Hamburgers? Cheeseburgers? Or how about my fabulous venison burgers? They're only four pounds fifty, and as you're a family I'll do you a special deal.'

'What's venison, Mummy?' Philip asked.

'Well it's erm...' mumbled Jumoke, making exaggerated shapes with her lips. 'It's kind of, erm ...this, erm...'

'It's deer, like Bambi,' I said which made Philip leap back from the van as though it had caught on fire.

'No, Mummy! I don't want to eat Bambi. Please don't make me eat it,' he started screeching.

'There's no need to be upset, Philip,' said Jumoke hugging him. 'Mummy won't make you eat the burger if you don't want to.'

'He's a bit sensitive, is Philip,' whispered Quincy in my ear. '*Bambi*'s also his favourite film.'

Poor Philip, I thought. I felt like giving him a hug myself. Casper, however, seemed determined to wind Philip up as much as he could.

'Can *I* eat Bambi, Mummy? I think Bambi's yum,' said Casper, which only made Philip more hysterical.

'It's all right, Philip, nobody's eating venison,' said Jumoke as he thrashed about in her arms. 'Casper will have an ordinary burger like everyone else.'

She stuck four fingers up at the man in the van. 'Four ordinary beef burgers, please.'

'Four ordinary beef burgers coming up,' he replied.

'It's all right Philip, Mummy's here,' said Jumoke as she rocked him like a baby. After a few minutes he stopped whining.

As soon as the man handed us the burgers Quincy, Casper and me tucked in like a pack of hungry wolves, Philip, though, nibbled cautiously; checking the inside of the bun every so often to make sure it definitely wasn't venison he was eating. Jumoke was the only one not eating a burger. Instead she was eating this funny-looking sandwich, which didn't look the least bit appetising.

'Rice cakes,' she said to me. 'I'm on a diet.'

Then she smiled. 'Quincy's been talking non-stop about coming to see you in your school play. I can't tell you how excited he is, Lolly.'

I gulped. I still hadn't decided how I was going to break it to Quincy that he couldn't come. I still wanted Dad to be there.

'So, do you enjoy acting?' asked Jumoke.

'Yes, I love it, but I'm not sure that I want to be an actress when I grow up. I might be an events manager like my mum as it seems like a really cool job, but I haven't totally made up my mind yet.'

Jumoke laughed. 'Oh, don't worry about that. You've got plenty of time before you start thinking about a career. You've still got school to get through first. Did you know I used to be an actress?'

'Did you?'

'Yes, did Quincy not tell you?'

I shook my head.

'I never quite made it to Hollywood, but I did get to appear in a few TV dramas,' said Jumoke.

'Wow! You're the first person I've met that's been on TV. So, how come you're not acting any more?'

'I guess I just got bored with it after a while, and I fancied doing something else. As cooking was something I enjoyed, I decided I'd set up my own catering business,' said Jumoke. 'That's how I met Quincy. He was putting on an event and was looking for a caterer, and he's been the love of my life ever since. By the way, Lolly, if you ever need any tips on acting, you can call me any time.'

'Thanks,' I replied gratefully. I just hoped my mum wouldn't mind.

After lunch we headed down to the beach.

'I'm going to build a sandcastle,' said Casper as he jumped about in the sand.

'But you don't have your bucket and spade,' said Philip. 'What will you build it with?'

'With my hands, dummy,' said Casper. 'Hey, why don't we have a competition to see who can build the best one?'

He looked at Quincy. 'Can you be the judge, Daddy?'

'Sure, I don't mind,' he said.

'Well, if you're going to build a sandcastle then I'm going to build a sand *palace*, and mine is going to be way better than yours,' Philip goaded his brother.

'No it won't,' said Casper. 'And, anyway, there's no such thing as a sand palace. Isn't that right, Daddy?'

'Actually, I think there might be some sand palaces out there, Casper, and if Philip wants to make one then that's absolutely fine.' He looked over at me. 'Would you like to join in, Lolly?'

'OK,' I shrugged and kneeled down in the sand.

Jumoke poured some water over each of our sand piles so we could mould them. I decided to do the Landsdale, but a prettier version. I'd never made a council estate out of sand before. It certainly was a challenge, but I was confident that it would beat Casper's sandcastle and Philip's palace. I started off by recreating the lawn – without all the junk and dog poo in it – rolling a little ball of sand, which would be a water fountain, and then rolling some other balls to make the flowers. Afterwards I began building my family's block, all fifteen storeys, using a dumped lollipop stick to smooth it out so it didn't look too wonky.

'I'm finished,' said Casper annoyingly, after just a short time. I'd only got to the third floor of the Landsdale. 'Who's won, Daddy?'

Quincy walked around us, a finger on his chin as he pretended to look thoughtful. 'They're all very good, so well done. But I think the person who's impressed me with their building the most is . . . Lolly!'

'Noooo!' roared Casper. 'My sandcastle's better than hers!'

His sandcastle wasn't bad, as it goes. It certainly was better than Philip's palace, but definitely no match for my estate.

'You did well, son, don't worry,' Quincy tried to assure him. 'Now, how's about I treat you to an ice cream?'

'Yes please,' chirped Casper, distracted. 'Can I get mine with a flake in it?'

'Sure you can, son,' replied Quincy. 'Philip, would you like an ice cream?'

'Yes, yes,' said Philip, nodding his head excitedly.

'And what can I get you, Lolly?' he asked.

'Um, I'll have an ice cream but with strawberry sauce on it,' I said.

'But I want strawberry sauce!' said Casper. 'She's copying me, Daddy.'

'No, I don't think she is, Casper, because you didn't actually say you wanted strawberry sauce. But if that's what you want I'll get them to put some on for you,' said Quincy and looked at Jumoke.

'No treats for me thanks,' she said to him. 'I'm watching my figure, remember.'

Quincy headed off to fetch our ice creams.

'Your castle's rubbish,' hissed Casper as I got up from the sand.

'No it's not,' I said. 'And it's not a castle, it's a tower block.'

Casper threw some sand at me. It went in my face and all over my yellow teddy bear. My eyes were stinging and before I knew it Casper had snatched my bear.

'I want the bear more than you,' he barked. 'He's mine.'

'No, he's mine!' I shouted, trying to pull it back from him. He suddenly stumbled and fell over, taking my bear with him. Tears sprang from his eyes.

'Mummy, Lolly pushed me!' he cried.

'What? She pushed you,' said Jumoke, walking over to Casper and giving him a hug. 'Is that true, Lolly, did you push him?' she asked me slowly.

'No, it's not true. I didn't touch him.'

'She's lying, Mummy. She did push me,' said Casper wailing wildly. I'm sure it was just an act to get me into trouble.

'I believe him, Mummy.' Philip gave me a nasty look. 'She pushed him.'

Jumoke frowned at me. 'But he's your little brother, Lolly, why would you want to hurt him?'

'I didn't!' I said, feeling like Little Miss Horrid even though I'd done nothing wrong.

'Hey, what's with the commotion?' Quincy asked. He'd come back minus our ice creams. 'The whole beach can hear you.'

'It's Lolly's fault, Daddy. She pushed me,' Casper shrieked.

'It's not true. I didn't push him,' I burbled.

'Now, you're not telling tales are you, Casper?' said Quincy.

'No, Daddy, I'm not. She did push me,' he sniffled. 'I hate Lolly. I hate her! She's horrible!'

'He doesn't mean that,' said Quincy quickly. He flashed me one of his stupid toothy grins.

'I do mean it, I hate her!' yelled Casper.

'Well I hate you too,' I thundered, feeling hurt. 'I hate all of you and I want to go home.'

Deep down, I didn't really hate them. All I wanted was for my brothers to like me, but I was the one crying now. Quincy tried to hug me, but I jerked my body away. 'Take me home! I want to go home!'

He looked shocked, but nodded.

'I do hope you'll come and visit us again,' said Jumoke when we got back to where Quincy had parked his car. 'And I'm sorry for telling you off, I was just worried about the boys. But it was nice to meet you.'

Well it wasn't nice meeting you, I felt like saying back, but I kept shtoom as I got into the car.

'Bye, Lolly,' said Casper and Philip together.

I thought they'd be happy to see the back of me, but their faces looked quite sad.

Quincy tried to start up a conversation as he drove me home, but I was having none of it.

'I don't want to talk to you,' I snapped, burying my head in my teddies.

When we reached the Landsdale I dashed out of the car, slamming the door behind me.

'Lolly!' Quincy called, winding down the window.

I turned and glowered at him.

'I'm glad you spent the day with us,' he said, his smile wobbling. 'I'm not sure why you're angry with me, but I would love it if we could meet up again. Like I said before, I want to be there for you, Lolly. I want to be your dad.'

'I've already got a dad!' I screamed, running into my block and not stopping until I reached the flat.

When I got in, I dropped my teddies onto the sofa and marched straight to my room. Zola was there, sitting on her bed crying.

'What's happened?' I asked, worried.

'It's Dad,' she whimpered. 'He phoned . . . he's going away, Lolly.'

'Going away!' I gasped, my hands shaking. 'Where?'

'To Birmingham,' said Zola miserably. 'He's going to live with Uncle Finn.'

'Does Mum know?'

She shook her head. 'No, she's gone round to

Auntie Louise's,' she said. 'Dad's going today, Lolly, and he's not coming back.'

'It's because of me, isn't it?' I murmured, tears pricking my eyes. 'He probably thinks I love Quincy more than I love him. I've hurt Dad, haven't I? I bet he's only leaving so he can get as far away from me as possible. He hates me, Zola.'

'Oh, not this again! He doesn't hate you, Lolly,' she said.

I looked at a paper fan on the wall. It was one I'd made ages ago, and on it was a picture I'd drawn of Mum, Dad, Zola and me.

'I wish things could be like how they used to be before I turned eleven,' I whispered, sighing deeply. 'It was on my birthday when things started to go wrong. Eleven must be an unlucky number because I was really lucky before that. But now I have no luck whatsoever.'

'I wish things could be like they were then too, but that's never going to happen now, is it? Not when Dad's moving away,' said Zola. 'And quit going on about not having any luck. It's getting boring now, Lolly.'

I headed to the door.

'I have to see him, Zola, tell him not to go. Do you remember the name of the road the B&B was on?'

'What are you doing? You can't go to the hotel,' said Zola. 'Mum would kill me if she knew I'd let you go wandering off on your own. And Dad's probably—'

'Kelmore Close, that's it,' I said, remembering. 'I'll get there faster if I go on my bike.'

'No, Lolly, stay here,' Said Zola. Then she looked at me suspiciously. 'And how come you're home so early? Mum said you wouldn't be back until after seven. What's going on?'

'I don't want to talk about it,' I said and hurried out the room.

Zola shouted at me to come back, but I took no notice. I needed to stop Dad from leaving. I grabbed my bike from the hallway and when I got outside I leaped on and began cycling as fast as I could.

Only I didn't manage to make it to the B&B. I didn't even make it to the other side of the road. I didn't see the car coming I only heard it, its screeching tyres as it slammed into my bike, followed by screams from people passing by as my body collided with the ground. Then everything went black. It seemed my luck really had gone, this time for good.

Chapter 12

As I opened my eyes, the first person I saw was Dad. I was no longer lying in the middle of the road but was in a hospital bed with the worst headache ever. Mum and Zola were there too crying.

'What happened?' I asked woozily.

'You had a very nasty accident,' replied my dad.

'You don't know how lucky you are, Lollipop,' Mum said, kissing the top of my head that was all bandaged up.

I groaned. 'My head, Mum, it hurts.'

'It will do, Lollipop,' said Dad. 'But don't worry, the doctor's going to give you something for the pain. Do you remember what happened?'

I tried to nod but my head was too sore. 'There was a car. It hit me.'

'You were knocked unconscious,' said Mum.

'We were so worried about you, sis,' Zola whispered.

'Am I going to be OK?' I murmured.

'You will be, thank heavens,' said Dad, 'but you really had us terrified, Lollipop. Fortunately you escaped with only a couple of cuts and bruises, but it could've been a lot worse.'

'I'm like Pollyanna,' I said. 'In the play she gets hit by a car.' Then I started to panic. 'Oh no! What if I'm not well enough to do the play? I'd hate not to be in it.'

'I'm sure you'll be back to normal in time for the play,' said Mum soothingly. 'But you will have to take it easy over the next few days.'

'I was coming to see you, Dad, that's why I was on my bike,' I remembered. 'I wanted to stop you from moving to Birmingham.'

'But I was never moving to Birmingham, Lollipop,' he whispered. 'It seems your sister got the wrong end of the stick. I was only going to stay with your uncle Finn for a few days. It wasn't going to be for ever.'

He glanced at Zola then looked back at me.

'I'd never want to be far away from you two. And, besides, I've got a new job to start.'

'You have a job? That's wonderful, Dad,' I said softly.

'I start next Monday,' he smiled. 'It's similar to what I was doing before, but it's a more senior position so I'll have more money coming in.'

'Well done, Dad!' I said, wincing as I struggled to sit up and give him a hug.

'Careful. You have to take it easy, remember?' he said hugging me back.

'I was really scared you'd stopped loving me, Dad, because I'm not your daughter, and that I'd made you upset by inviting Quincy to the play.'

'You *are* my daughter, Lolly, and I love you more than you'll ever know. And I'm not upset you invited Quincy to your play. That's just who you are – friendly and kind – and that's why I love you.' His eyes filled with tears. 'All I care about is that you're here, alive, my little Lollipop.'

He kissed my hand. 'You and Zola are all that matter to me, and from now on I'll be making sure that I'm around for the both of you.'

'So does that mean you're coming home? Are you and Mum back together?' I asked.

Dad stroked my head gently.

'No, Lollipop, we're not back together,' he said slowly. 'But last night your mother and I had a long heart to heart, didn't we?'

Mum nodded.

'Your accident has made us see how much our separation has affected you girls,' said Dad. 'We've both been very selfish these past few weeks and too wrapped up in own our troubles to notice that we were upsetting you and your sister. I haven't stopped loving your mum, but there are issues that we both know that we need to resolve.'

'We've agreed to go and see this person called a marriage counsellor,' said Mum. 'Someone who'll help us sort out the problems in our relationship, and we'll just take things from there.'

My heart did a little flip. Maybe my prayers would be answered. Maybe we'd all be a family again.

'But I do want to be nearer to you and Zola,' said Dad. 'So I'm going to look at renting a flat near the Landsdale.'

Just then Dad's mobile rang. He answered it. 'It's my new boss,' he whispered. 'He just wants to confirm a start time for next week.' He left the room.

'Quincy and your brothers send their love,' said Mum. 'Quincy said that Casper and Philip are very sorry about how they behaved when you met up and that they would all love to see you again.'

'I'd like to see them too, but maybe I shouldn't, Mum. I might hurt Dad's feelings. And perhaps I should tell Quincy not to come to the play even though Dad says he doesn't mind.'

'Who doesn't mind?' said Dad, coming back into the room.

'Are you sure you're fine with Quincy coming to my play?' I asked him tentatively.

'Yes, Lollipop, I am,' he replied, holding my hand. 'Quincy's a part of your life now, I accept that and I won't be trying to prevent him from getting to know you. But what we will be doing is taking care of you. We all want to make sure you get better.'

I left the hospital the following day. I had a few days off school while I recovered at home with Mum and Dad fussing over me the whole time. But I enjoyed it, and it was good having Dad around. He came over every evening after work, making the dinner sometimes, as well as helping me rehearse my lines for the play.

Things were definitely different between him and Mum. It was like they'd suddenly become two people who'd only just met. And Dad was acting like he'd never lived at the flat, he was always asking where things were even though he knew the answer.

When I got back to school there was only one more rehearsal before the play. Mr Scott was really impressed with my acting, but he still reckoned I needed an understudy and he'd given the job to Dominique Foster while I was away. I was adamant that I didn't need her, but I was relieved that my understudy wasn't Mariella. She still got to play Mrs Tarbell, although when her parents found out she'd cheated in the English test they refused to let her have a rabbit.

When the actual night of the play arrived I was dead nervous, especially when I sneaked a peek through the stage curtains and saw all the people in the audience. Then I glimpsed some familiar faces: my mum and dad, Zola, Jumoke, who'd come with Quincy, and also Mrs Avery, which made me feel even more nervous. I guess it was because I wanted to make them proud, and I did.

The play was a huge success. I didn't forget any of my lines and everyone said my acting was superb. I made Mr Scott cry again and I even spotted Mr Kingsley wiping a tear from his eye at one point.

At the end we got a long round of applause and several whoops as we took a bow.

Mum and Dad gave me a big hug afterwards and Quincy and Jumoke came over to congratulate me too. It was a tense moment as my two dads came face to face, but they were both polite, shaking hands and exchanging small talk about the traffic on the high street and the hot weather.

The last day of school was an emotional day as my class said goodbye to each other, and to Maple Lane School. For me it did feel scary knowing I wouldn't be coming back and that I'd be moving on to high school, with new faces and subjects. But at least I'd have Nancy with me, and I'd get to see Zola there every day.

Mrs Avery came in to say goodbye and she brought little Oliver with her. Mariella was desperate to hold him and was boasting about how she knew everything there was to know about babies just because her mum's a midwife. Mrs Avery did let her hold him, but I don't think Oliver wanted to be held by Mariella because as soon as she took him he puked up all over her. Everyone in my class thought it was hilarious. Mariella didn't, though, and she bolted off like a horse to the toilets to clean the sick off her clothes.

In the evening my class had a disco in the school hall. The DJ played loads of Corey T songs, which made me very happy. Nancy was happy too, but that was more to do with the fact that she got to dance with Kofi. But I don't think they're going to be boyfriend and girlfriend just yet. Nancy says she wants to 'keep her options open' in case there are more cute boys at our high school.

I spent heaps of time at Nancy's house during the holidays, which was fab because I got to play loads with Cheese and Pickle, and help Nancy make cupcakes. I also met up with Quincy and my brothers. One day we went to the cinema and then the second time we met up we drove down to London and went on the London Eye and visited Madame Tussauds. I had a really good time, but the best thing about it was that my brothers were really nice to me. When we went to the cinema Casper let me share his popcorn and I let him have some of my nachos. And when we went on the London Eye Philip asked me to hold his hand when he started feeling dizzy.

Even though I'll always see Dad as my proper dad, I'm really enjoying getting to know Quincy and I'm planning to meet up with him and my brothers some more. In the meantime we've been chatting regularly on the phone.

I've also been helping Mum to redecorate the flat with Zola and Dad. It's been great fun. The new wallpaper in the living room is so pretty, and my and Zola's bedroom has been painted in this lovely peach colour.

When Dad found a flat we all helped him get settled in and we went shopping with him for furniture. It was like we were all a family again, only Dad wasn't living with us.

I still hope that one day my parents will get back together, and fingers crossed that day will be soon. It's certainly been a weird few months, but despite all the things that have happened – Dad losing his job, moving to the Landsdale, Dad leaving, meeting my real father and half brothers, my accident – I've stopped wishing for things to go back to how they were before my eleventh birthday. I'm happy with things as they are now because I'm surrounded by people who love me very much; people who make me feel like the luckiest girl in the world.

The End

Acknowledgements

Special thanks to my editor, Charlie Sheppard, and my agent, Eve White. A big thank you also goes to my cousin Saffron Hamilton for her suggestions and advice throughout the writing of my novel.

About the Author

Born and raised in London, where she still lives today, Ellie Daines always aspired to one day become an author, and as a child she spent much of her spare time writing short stories. At university, Ellie studied journalism and then later spent several years working in online marketing for various companies.

To find out more about Ellie Daines visit her website: www.elliedaines.com

Abela

BERLIE DOHERTY

Two girls.

Abela lives in an African village and has lost everything. What will be her fate as an illegal immigrant? Will she find a family in time?

'I don't want a sister or brother,' thinks Rosa in England. Could these two girls ever become sisters?

Abela is the powerful and moving story of a true heroine who overcomes great hardship. Double Carnegie-winning author Berlie Doherty writing at her very best.

Shortlisted for the Manchester Book Award, the Coventry Inspiration Book Award 2009 and The Blue Peter Book Awards.

'Excellent . . . what could be an unbearably sad tale is made compulsively readable by a writer of grace and skill.' *Independent*

HBK 9781842706893 £10.99
PBK 9781842707258 £5.99

When You Reach Me

Rebecca Stead

Miranda's life is starting to unravel. Her best friend, Sal, gets punched by a kid on the street for what seems like no reason, and he shuts Miranda out of his life. Then the key Miranda's mum keeps hidden for emergencies is stolen, and a mysterious note arrives:

'I am coming to save your friend's life, and my own. I ask two favours. First, you must write me a letter.'

The notes keep coming, and whoever is leaving them knows things no one should know. Each message brings her closer to believing that only she can prevent a tragic death. Until the final note makes her think she's too late.

Winner of the John Newbery Medal 2010

Shortlisted for the Waterstone's Children's Book Prize

'Smart and mesmerising'
New York Times

9781849392129 £5.99